"I'm going to kill you," Adler said in the same tightly controlled, fury-driven voice. "You know that."

Clayburn didn't believe it. Didn't believe Adler was man enough to face him evenly, no matter how crazy with anger he was.

There was the blank wall of the saloon on Clayburn's right. He turned his head swiftly and looked to his left.

Wilks was there, standing in an opening between two tents. His left arm was in a sling. There was a Colt in his right hand, pointing. . . .

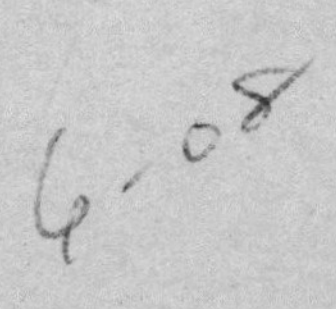

Also by Marvin Albert:

THE UNTOUCHABLES

Published by Fawcett Books:

Stone Angel Series:

STONE ANGEL

BACK IN THE REAL WORLD

GET OFF AT BABYLON

LONG TEETH

THE LAST SMILE

Gold Medal Classic Westerns:

APACHE RISING

RIDER FROM WIND RIVER

THE REFORMED GUN

Tony Rome Mysteries:

MIAMI MAYHEM

THE LADY IN CEMENT

LAST TRAIN TO BANNOCK

Marvin H. Albert

FAWCETT GOLD MEDAL • NEW YORK

A Fawcett Gold Medal Book
Published by Ballantine Books
 Published in the United States by Ballantine Books, a division of Random House, Inc., New York, and simultaneously in Canada by Random House of Canada Limited, Toronto. Originally published by Dell Publishing Co., Inc., in 1963.

ISBN 0-449-13383-4

Manufactured in the United States of America

First Ballantine Books Edition: September 1989

ONE

The stagecoach carrying the man they'd been hired to kill was not in sight yet. They sat their horses among the rocks on the jagged crest of the hill and gazed north along the route down which it would be coming on its way to Parrish City. The road snaked emptily toward them through a sun-scorched, barren land of eroded buttes and wind-rippled sand dunes. Except for an occasional dust devil there was nothing moving between the waiting killers and the horizon.

Snow gleamed on the peaks of the far-distant mountains. It was well into fall. But they'd ridden hard all morning, and this far south the sun was still strong enough to take its toll of men and horses.

"No telling how long it'll be till that stage shows up," grumbled Pollock, a heavy, harsh-faced man in his late twenties. "May have to wait here the rest of the day."

"So we'll wait," Wilks told him flatly. His stocky figure slouched in the saddle as he surveyed the distances, his arrogant, mocking blue eyes squinted against the blazing sun. Wilks was the youngest of the three men. His two days' growth of beard showed as soft red-gold fuzz. But he was unmistakably the leader of the trio.

Pollock scratched his bristly black stubble and tugged his hat forward to shade his eyes more. "Harry Farnell better be aboard like he's supposed to be. Or we've had a lot of riding for nothing."

"Farnell's due in Parrish by tonight," Wilks pointed out. "And there's just the one stage through today."

"Maybe he won't come by stage. Could be he decided to ride south on his own, like we did."

"Could be," Wilks acknowledged carelessly. "But why would he? Farnell ain't expecting trouble."

He took off his hat, revealing a tangled thatch of red hair, and wiped a hand across his wide forehead. Shaking drops of sweat from his thick, stubby fingers, he glanced at the third man, Ryle, a lean old-timer with a seamed, leathery face.

"No sense us all baking our brains out," he told Ryle with easy authority. "You settle here and keep watch. We'll be down at the stage station. If that stage don't show in a couple hours I'll send Pollock up to relieve you."

Ryle, some twenty-five years older than Wilks, accepted his order without question. He merely nodded, climbed off his horse, and found himself a patch of shade between two boulders from which he had a clear view of the road. Wilks turned his mount and headed south toward the small stage station huddled out of sight at the foot of the hills.

Pollock followed and caught up with him. For a few moments he rode in silence beside Wilks. Then he spoke up carefully, out of deference to the younger man's judgment. "I sure hope you're right about Farnell bein' on the stage. If he gets to Parrish, we don't get paid."

Wilks grinned boyishly. "He'll get to Parrish, all right. Only not alive."

Clayburn reached the stage station on foot, carrying his saddle gear across his shoulder and the twelve-shot Winchester .44 carbine in his left hand. Alkali dust was caked thick on his clothes and formed a mask on his lean, strong-boned face. The sun had baked him dry and his long legs were heavy with fatigue. His boots had not been designed for hours of hiking across rough country.

He paused next to a tangle of rock and cactus, his wide-spread greenish eyes taking in the buildings by the road—an adobe shack and a small barn. There were three horses in the rope corral, grouped close in the patch of dark shade thrown by the barn wall. With a sigh of relief, Clayburn strode on toward the open-doored shack.

Inside, Wilks, Pollock and the station manager were around the table playing poker. Wilks had seated himself where he could watch through the open door and single window. He was the first to notice the approach of the tall, wide-shouldered, lanky man. He noted the stranger's battered slouch hat, old buckskin shirt and well-worn Levis, and pegged him for a cowhand.

"Company coming," he announced.

The plump, middle-aged station manager turned in his chair and looked. "What d'you know. Walkin' . . ." He placed his cards facedown, shoved to his feet and went out to meet the newcomer.

"Looks like you've had trouble," he greeted Clayburn amiably.

"My horse broke a leg yesterday afternoon. Any chance of buying one of yours?"

The station manager shook his head. "Only got one."

Clayburn glanced toward the corral.

"Them other two ain't mine," the station manager explained. "Belong to a couple fellows just taking a rest inside before riding on. But there's a stage coming through today. Going on south to Parrish City. Whereabouts you headed?"

"Parrish'll do. When's the stage expected?"

"Now. Which might mean three hours from now."

When Clayburn smiled it softened the set of his wide mouth and crinkles appeared through the dust at the corners of his eyes. "Time enough. I could use a wash. So could my clothes. Been a long walk."

"Cost you a dollar."

The price was reasonable. A man could expect a free drink, but water for anything else came dear in the southwest. He nodded. "I've got a dollar."

From inside the shack, Wilks and Pollock watched Clayburn follow the plump man into the barn.

"He could be a problem," Pollock said.

The young redhead shrugged. "Any extra gun's an extra problem. But he'll be easy enough to take care of."

He told Pollock how, briefly, before the station manager returned from the barn.

Left alone in the barn with a cut-down barrel half filled with water, Clayburn dropped his hat and gunbelt next to the carbine and saddlebags, pulled off his boots. Before tugging out of his shirt he glanced at the doorway to make sure no one was observing him. The left sleeve had concealed a narrow-bladed knife in a soft buckskin sheath strapped to the inside of his forearm.

He'd first taken to wearing it back when he'd been one of the New Mexico agents for Colonel Remsberg's detective agency. It had come in handy often enough to teach him the wisdom of continuing to wear it after he'd quit the Colonel. For a man who now earned his way mostly with a deck of cards, it was a form of insurance.

Unstrapping the knife, he got out of the rest of his clothes and slammed them against a post till he'd knocked off most of the hard-caked dust. After washing himself, he soaked the clothes in the barrel and wrung them out. Then he got his town clothes from his saddlebags. When he was dressed, he carried the wet clothing out of the barn and spread it on a humped rock to dry in the sun.

When he entered the adobe shack the three men around the table stared at him. He didn't look the same man. He wore black, relieved only by a gold cravat setting off the darkness of his linen shirt, and the bone grip of his holstered Colt. His flat-crowned Stetson was an expensive one, and the broadcloth of his trousers and open frock coat had obviously been cut to measure by a good tailor.

Wilks quickly revised his original estimate of Clayburn. Whatever the stranger was, he wasn't any ordinary cowhand. Clothes like that meant money—and Wilks prided himself on his poker skill. He used his boyish grin on the tall man. "Want to sit in? Pass the time till the stage comes."

"Good a way as any," Clayburn agreed, and took the only empty chair, across the table from the burly Pollock.

Little more than half an hour later Pollock and the station manager were out of the game, broke. They sat in their chairs disgustedly as the game became a two-man duel. Over the stretch of played hands Wilks had won most often, but Clayburn had raked in the biggest pots. The young redhead concentrated on reversing this trend, without success. Five deals later, most of the money on the table was in front of Clayburn.

Wilks was no longer smiling. He watched narrow-eyed as Clayburn dealt, noting how the cards, flicked out with apparent carelessness by the long, rope-scarred fingers, fell exactly into place one on top of the other. His eyes remained on Clayburn as he began picking up his hand.

"I've sure been dumb," he said tightly.

"No," Clayburn told him. "You play a smart game. It's just the way the cards are running."

"I mean I sized you up wrong," Wilks snapped. "You're a gambler, ain't you?"

"I've played a lot of poker," Clayburn conceded with a faint smile.

He'd been winning because he'd found Wilks easy to read. Now he was waiting for the redhead to lose his temper, and sensed that he was close to it. But Wilks, after a glance at his cards, simmered down and opened for ten dollars. Which meant that he had a strong enough hand to check his growing anger.

Clayburn's hand consisted of a pair of sixes, a pair of queens, and a nine. He saw the ten-dollar bet, not raising, and discarded the nine. Wilks also threw away one card, but Clayburn decided it would have required more than two pairs to control Wilks' temper.

He dealt Wilks a card, picked off one for himself. He'd acquired a jack, not improving his two pairs at all. Wilks was studying his cards, making a show of having difficulty deciding how to play them.

Finally Wilks shrugged. "Might as well give you the rest of my dough." He shoved all of his remaining cash into the center of the table with the original twenty.

" 'Fraid you've got me beat." Without expression, Clayburn folded his hand.

Wilks was furious. He'd had three kings to start with, had kept an ace and acquired another—for a full house. And all it had earned him was ten dollars from Clayburn. With an effort, he forced a grin. "You sure bluff easy."

"Oh?" Clayburn said innocently. "Were you bluffing?"

"Yeah."

"Joke's on me, then. Your deal."

Wilks raked in the pot and started shuffling the cards. This time Clayburn acquired only a pair of jacks. He opened for ten dollars. Wilks instantly saw him and raised it another ten dollars, still forcing the grin. Clayburn read Wilks as intending to follow a pretended bluff with a real one. He saw the raise and discarded three cards. Wilks discarded only one, then dealt three to Clayburn and one to himself.

Clayburn had picked up another jack, making it three of a kind. He bet another ten dollars. Without a moment's hesitation, Wilks saw the bet and raised it with everything he had left. His grin seemed pasted on his face now. Clayburn studied him for a moment, then counted the cash from his pile and dropped it on the pot. "See you."

Wilks' grin crumpled. He flung his cards on the table, face up, showing only a pair of tens. Clayburn spread out his own cards and set himself for an explosion.

The explosion didn't come. There was the sound of an approaching horse outside. Wilks turned his head quickly, looking through the doorway.

The station manager got to his feet and went to the door. "Looks like this is my day not to be lonely."

Wilks got up and went to the window. "Man on a spotted horse," he said quietly, and turned to face the interior of the room again. His hand blurred with motion, sweeping the gun out of his holster.

Clayburn saw the beginning of the move and went for his own gun. He didn't get a chance to find out if he'd have beaten the redhead to the draw. Pollock shoved his heavy bulk against the table, ramming it into Clayburn and overturning him with his chair. Clayburn hit the floor hard, twisted, and came up on one knee, gripping the butt of his Colt. But by then Wilks had dead aim on him, and Pollock had drawn his gun, too.

Clayburn opened his fingers, letting the Colt slide back into the holster as he rose to his feet. The station manager backed against the inside wall, whispering, "What is this?" But he knew what it was. He already had his hands up, making no effort to go for his own revolver.

Wilks relieved him of it, and kept both guns steady on Clayburn as Pollock moved around behind the tall gambler and took his Colt. He shoved it into his belt.

The leathery faced Ryle appeared in the doorway. "Stage coming," he told Wilks.

Wilks nodded without taking his eyes from Clayburn. "Get all the horses inside the barn. Then stay out of sight and cover from there."

As Ryle vanished, Wilks advanced to the table. Putting down the station manager's gun, his free hand began picking up the money and stuffing it into his pockets. "Looks like I win after all, gambler."

Clayburn stared back at him without expression.

Wilks pocketed the last of Clayburn's winnings. "Maybe you figure it belongs to you? I say you were cheating, tinhorn."

Clayburn merely continued to look at him, his face wooden.

His failure to show any reaction enraged Wilks. With a vicious tightening of his face, the redhead slammed his gun at Clayburn's head.

Clayburn moved as the heavy gun barrel caught him in the temple. He saved himself from the full force of the blow, but it was still bad enough to drop him to the floor against the wall with his senses spinning and pain lashing through his brain.

"Get over by the window," Wilks snapped at Pollock. As the heavy man obeyed, Wilks broke open the station manager's gun and dumped all the cartridges. He closed the revolver, went to the station manager and shoved it back in his holster. "Now when the stagecoach pulls up, you go out there and act like nothing's wrong. Understand?"

The station manager nodded quickly, tried to speak and found he couldn't.

"You better," Wilks told him flatly. " 'Less you want your spine broke by a bullet."

"We oughta kill him and the gambler now," Pollock said. "Make the job that much easier when the stage . . ."

"I'm running this!" Wilks snarled. "And I say we'll wait and make sure Farnell's on that stage first. If he ain't, there's no point in killing anybody else. Having the law on our tail for murder—without even gettin' paid for it."

Clayburn remained sprawled on the floor with his shoulders against the wall, fighting against dizziness and the blurring of his vision. The sound of the approaching stagecoach reached him. He raised his right hand and gently touched the swollen bruise on the side of his head. He let the hand fall so that its fingers touched the cuff of his left sleeve.

Neither Wilks nor Pollock saw anything in that to alarm them.

TWO

The plump station manager came out of the adobe shack as the stage pulled to a jangling, screeching halt in front of it. His empty gun was in his holster, his hands hung down at his sides, and he was trying to smile as ordered. But he moved as though stepping on eggs.

The big man riding shotgun up beside the team driver raised a hand in greeting. "Hi, Arnie. How late are we?"

The station manager had to work his throat open to get the words out. " 'Bout an hour." He lost his struggle to keep the smile on his face. There was in him a need to break through his fear, shout a warning and throw himself to the ground. But it was a small need alongside the massive awareness of the two men hidden inside the shack with guns aimed at his back.

Numbly, he watched the driver lock the brake and tie the reins, saw the coach door open and the three passengers—all men—start climbing out to stretch their legs.

Wilks came out of the doorway behind the station manager. Pollock appeared inside the window, dividing his attention between Clayburn and the men outside, ready to turn his gun in either direction, as needed. Clayburn braced his heavy shoulders against the wall and waited, his head lolling to one side as though he were still semiconscious. The mist in front of his eyes was beginning to dissolve, and the tips of his fingers were now inside the left sleeve of his coat.

Outside, Wilks shoved the station manager out of his

way and smiled at one of the passengers who'd climbed out of the coach—a middle-aged businessman with a solid build going thick around the middle.

"Hello, Farnell . . ."

The second Harry Farnell recognized Wilks and saw the gun in his hand he knew what was coming. His hand vanished under his coat, grabbing desperately for the small revolver he kept there.

Wilks laughed softly and the gun in his hand roared. The slug rammed into Farnell's chest, driving him back against the coach and pinning him there for a split second. As he crumpled toward the ground the man riding shotgun—he actually carried a rifle—broke out of his stupor and twisted in his high seat, bringing his rifle around to bear on the red-haired killer.

Before he could squeeze the trigger Ryle's rifle crashed out from inside the barn. The bullet caught the shotgun rider in the head, killing him instantly. His rifle spilled from lifeless hands and fell as he sagged back in the high seat next to the stage driver, his head tipping back, sightless eyes staring at the sky. The team horses, frightened by the crash of gunfire, reared and whinnied, but the driver caught the reins and held them steady. The other two passengers had already thrown their hands high and were standing there frozen, eager to give no one an excuse for shooting at them.

It was all over that quickly. Or seemed to be. Wilks stood holding his Colt carelessly, gazing down at the still figure of Farnell in the dust before him. Ryle was walking from the barn toward the shack, rifle still ready in both hands.

Inside the shack Pollock took his eyes off Clayburn and called through the window to Wilks, "Might as well lift whatever the passengers got on 'em while we're . . ."

Clayburn came to life in the same instant, drawing the knife out of his sleeve and throwing it in the same motion as he lunged to his feet.

Pollock whipped around, trying to shoot Clayburn and dodge the flung knife at the same time. He succeeded in neither. The knifeblade plunged into his chest, cutting off his scream as it started. He squeezed the trigger automatically as he fell forward. The gun boomed within the confines of the small room, the slug chopping into the adobe wall.

Clayburn reached Pollock as his body hit the dirt floor. Snatching his own Colt from the dead man's belt, he straightened beside the window, ready to fire through it at Wilks.

But the redhead had reacted fast to the sound of Pollock's gun inside the shack. By the time Clayburn reached the window Wilks was holding one of the passengers between him and the shack, using the man as a shield. When he spotted Clayburn he instantly began backing toward the barn, dragging his terrified shield along with him. He saw no sense in running the risk of trying to shoot it out. His mission was accomplished; he'd get paid. Now he was concentrating on getting away.

But Ryle, halfway between the barn and the shack, spotted Clayburn too, and decided he could get him. He snapped up his rifle, taking aim at the window. As he fired, Clayburn took a step backward into deeper shadow. The rifle bullet slashed past his ear as he fired his own aimed Colt. The distance wasn't good. The slug got Ryle in the hip, staggering him, but he didn't go down.

Clayburn was taking aim again when another shot sounded from next to the stagecoach. The plump station manager had gone down on one knee and seized the rifle dropped by the dead shotgun rider. It was his shot that killed Ryle.

While the rifle shot still echoed, Wilks fired from behind his human shield. The station manager fell back with a scream of pain, clutching his bullet-broken shoulder. Wilks continued backing toward the barn, one hand gripping the back of his prisoner's coat, too well hidden behind the other man for Clayburn to try a shot at him.

Leaving the window, he moved swiftly to the door. He slid his Colt back in its holster, crouched low, and dodged out toward the rifle the moaning station manager had dropped. Wilks' bullet kicked dirt against his leg as he reached and grabbed it. Clayburn dodged back to the protection of the corner of the adobe shack.

"Anybody tries to stop me," Wilks yelled, "and I shoot this pilgrim in the head!"

Clayburn levered a fresh shell into the rifle's fire chamber and took aim, hoping the man being used as a shield would have the sense to drop and give him a safe shot at the redhead's face. But it was a lost hope. The man's face was blank with shock and terror. His big figure continued to block Wilks from view the rest of the way to the barn.

Clayburn stayed where he was, waiting to get a shot at Wilks when he emerged. Two shots sounded inside the barn. Seconds later two horses raced out of the other end of the barn, headed for the hills to the north. Wilks was riding one and leading the other. And he had his hostage up on the first horse clinging to his back, still shielding him.

With a soft, vicious curse, Clayburn sprinted to the barn. Inside he found what he'd expected. The two horses left behind were dead.

Coming out of the barn, he watched Wilks riding fast up the nearest hill. At the top, without stopping the red-haired killer turned in his saddle and clubbed his gun against his hostage's head. The man fell backward from the horse and rolled part way down the slope. Before Clayburn could fire, Wilks and his two horses disappeared down the other side of the hill.

Clayburn lowered his rifle and glanced toward the stage and the shack. The station manager leaned against the wall, and the remaining passenger had begun trying to do what he could for the plump man's shoulder wound. Clayburn was surprised to see the stage driver sitting on the ground with Farnell's head on his lap.

Hurrying to them, he saw that Farnell was not yet dead—though he was getting closer to it by the second. His blood-smeared chest was heaving weakly and his eyes were glazed. Pink froth bubbled between his white lips as he tried to speak.

"What's he saying?" Clayburn asked the stage driver.

"Can't make it out. Something about hired killers is all I got so far."

Clayburn knelt over the dying man. "Who hired them?"

Farnell made an effort to answer. Broken sounds came out of him, but nothing intelligible.

Clayburn bent closer. "Who hired those men to kill you? Do you know?"

Farnell's lips twisted as he tried to get the words out. The only ones that could be understood were: ". . . bastard . . . said . . . he'd stop me . . ."

"Who?" Clayburn repeated insistently.

But this time there was no answer of any kind. Farnell stopped making the effort. His head rolled against the stage driver's knee and was still. He'd finished his dying.

Clayburn stood up and began trudging out to the unconscious man on the side of the hill.

THREE

The stagecoach took six hours to reach Parrish. On the way Clayburn rode up beside the driver and learned what he knew about Harry Farnell. Clayburn's interest was strictly personal. The red-haired killer had robbed him of his stake and his winnings. And pistol-whipped him into the bargain. These were things for which due retribution would be extracted. About such matters Clayburn had the persistence and patience of an Apache. And he figured the best method of finding the redhead was through whoever had hired him to do the killing.

According to the stage driver, Farnell had run a freight line out of Parrish. He'd hit a string of bad luck and been close to going out of business when he'd acquired a new partner recently who'd injected fresh money into his firm. The reason Farnell hadn't been able to weather his business losses on his own was that he'd sunk all the profits of his previous successful years into a big spread up north. That was where Farnell had been coming back from on the stage; his wife and children lived on the spread.

The stage driver couldn't think of anyone with a reason to hire killers to murder Farnell.

"How about this new partner of his?"

The driver shook his head. "Remember when he was tryin' to tell us who hired them? He said the *bastard* hired 'em. Never heard anybody call a woman a bastard. Some get called a lot of other things. But not that."

"Farnell's partner is a woman?"

"Uh-huh. Don't know much about her except she's mighty good-looking. Makes you sweat just to look at her. That kind. She ain't from anywhere around here. Name's Cora Sorel."

The name brought back a memory. Clayburn leaned back on the hard, jouncing seat, gazing thoughtfully past the pulling horses, across the flat distances to the southern horizon.

He didn't know much about Coral Sorel either. But he knew more than the stage driver.

It was dark when they got into Parrish, a big boomtown sprawled across the railroad tracks that cut through the Jemson Valley. Clayburn knew the place only from what he'd heard about it. Parrish had sprung up when the railroad first began pushing through the Valley, and for a couple years it had been the worst hell-spot in the Territory. But its lawless stage was past, ended by a town-taming marshal named Kavanaugh.

Parrish was still a wild enough place, with a flourishing red-light district. But now Marshal Kavanaugh, his tough-reputation deputies and a sheriff strong enough to handle the surrounding county kept the wildness under rigid control, confining the red-light goings on to an allotted section of town.

Within minutes of reaching Parrish, Clayburn had met the marshal and the sheriff. Both lived up to their reputations for efficiency. The wounded station manager was immediately turned over to a doctor, the bodies of the shotgun rider and Harry Farnell to the undertaker. The two passengers—one with a sizeable lump on his head—were questioned and allowed to register into the hotel. Twenty minutes after the stage came in, the sheriff rode out with a posse of six picked men to hunt down the red-haired killer.

Clayburn didn't think much of their chances. They wouldn't be able to start tracking the redhead till dawn. He wouldn't even have to concentrate on losing his trail so he couldn't be followed. With that much head start, and two horses for speed, he could get beyond the sheriff's jurisdiction before the posse got anywhere near him. If he wanted to do it that way. He'd been heading northwest the last Clayburn had seen of him. That way lay Indian territory and land that still had no law. All he had to do was keep going.

While Marshal Kavanaugh went off to talk to Farnell's partner, one of his deputies took Clayburn and the stage driver to the jailhouse office. They looked at the pictures on a stack of wanted posters that had come in from all over the southwest during the past couple of years.

They finished going through the stack, without spotting any picture or description that fitted the red-haired killer, by the time Marshal Kavanaugh returned. He was a big, raw-boned man with a florid face dominated by the kind of eyes to be expected in a man who'd tamed four hell-towns in succession over the past ten years.

"Any luck?" he asked in a friendly, businesslike voice that didn't go with his eyes.

His deputy shook his head. "Cora Sorel have any notion who the redhead is?"

"Nope. Nor who hired him. She says."

"Somebody," Clayburn said quietly, "must have some ideas about it."

Marshal Kavanaugh eyed him thoughtfully for a moment, sizing him up. "Sure, people've got suspicions. Lots of 'em, all going in different directions and not worth a damn. I got a couple myself. Both of which are probably wrong."

"I'd like to hear them, anyway."

The marshal shook his head. "Suspicions aren't proof. Making accusing statements without proof's against the law."

The stage driver spoke up. "Can I go now, marshal? I ain't needed a drink so bad in a long time."

Marshal Kavanaugh nodded. The driver unbuckled his gunbelt and left it on the desk. As he hurried out, the marshal turned to Clayburn.

"I'll take yours, too. Only lawmen are allowed to carry weapons in Parrish."

"You must have a real peaceful town."

Kavanaugh grunted. "Ain't had a quiet night in Parrish since I came here. Men got a right to let off steam, long as they do it in the right part of town. I don't care what they do to each other with their fists, boots or anything else they can get hold of—long as it doesn't start a riot or break up too much property. But weapons mean killing. And killing usually means the city has to pay for burial. Taxpayers don't like that."

Clayburn took off his gun belt, put it with his carbine on the marshal's desk.

Kavanaugh went on eying him. "The rule includes concealed knives, Clayburn."

His tone was deliberately quiet and not intended to give offense. His past ten years testified to his readiness to stand up against all kinds of men. But it also testified to his ability to judge men. He'd already decided that Clayburn was not the kind of man he'd care to tangle with, unless forced to it.

"Those men that were after Farnell thought they'd disarmed you," he went on quietly. "But you came up with a knife from someplace."

"I hope," Clayburn said just as quietly, "that you're this careful about everybody that comes into your city."

Marshal Kavanaugh nodded. "I got a collection of derringers and knives in that closet to prove it. Nobody fancies thirty days in the quarry digging rock for the new town hall. And that's the penalty for carrying any concealed weapon inside city limits. Penalty for using one is hanging."

"Hung many?"

"Some. None lately, though."

A suggestion of a smile touched the corners of Clayburn's mouth. He pulled up the left sleeve of his frock coat, unbuttoned and rolled up his shirt sleeve.

The marshal looked at the knife strapped in its sheath to the inside of Clayburn's forearm, hilt toward his wrist, "So that's where you had it."

Clayburn unstrapped the knife and put it down beside

his holstered Colt. "I may be back for the guns. If I find somebody that'll pay me enough for them to last me through a few hands of poker. That redhead just about cleaned me out."

"You want to eat meanwhile," Marshal Kavanaugh said, "you can get a meal at Henry's Diner, around the corner. Tell 'em I said to put it on my bill. I figure you earned it, out there at the stage station."

"Thanks. Where can I find Cora Sorel?"

"Princess Hotel. Up the street." Marshal Kavanaugh indicated the direction with his thumb. He asked no questions about why Clayburn wanted to know. But his eyes were thoughtful again as they followed him out of the jailhouse and up the street.

The Princess Hotel was the best in prosperous Parrish, and its carpeted lobby showed it. Learning that Cora Sorel had just gone into the hotel dining room, Clayburn went in and spotted her alone at one of the corner tables, studying the menu.

She was exactly as he remembered her. Though he'd only seen her once before, and that time briefly, Cora Sorel was not a woman a man could forget easily. She was dark-haired, with bold, beautiful lips and a knowing, sensuous kind of loveliness. There was slim strength in the assured way in which she held herself and moved. Only her dress was different from the last time he'd seen her. It looked like a French import. It was cut modestly enough, but the material, its darkness matching her hair, clung softly to her curves, flaunting them. She had a figure that didn't need much help at flaunting itself.

Cora Sorel looked up as he approached her table. Lustrous dark eyes took his measure, found him interesting.

Clayburn took off his black hat, "Good evening, Miss Sorel. My name's Clayburn. I was around when your partner got himself killed."

Her interest in him became more definite. "The marshal told me about you. That was quite a thing you did. Won't you join me for dinner?"

"I'm broke."

"My treat, then. Or would a woman buying you a meal offend your manliness?"

"I don't know about my manliness, but my stomach wouldn't mind at all."

As he seated himself across the table from her, a waiter came over. Cora Sorel ordered and passed the menu to Clayburn. She studied him as he ordered. When the waiter was gone she said, "Marshal Kavanaugh thinks you're a gambler. Are you?"

He nodded. "And how have the cards been running for *you*, lately?"

She leaned back a little in her chair, surprised. "You know me from some place?"

"I saw you once a couple of years back in a gambling house in San Francisco. Bucking the biggest poker game in the place." He smiled at her. "As I recall, you were winning pretty steadily."

Her beautifully curved lips quirked. "I usually manage to win more than I lose."

"Uh-huh. A good-looking woman is a natural draw for the big-money suckers."

She smiled at him more fully. "So we're both in the same line of business. How nice."

"I heard you'd changed your line. Gone into freighting."

"Thats strictly a one-time thing. Harry Farnell made me a proposition too good to pass up." Her face clouded as she named her dead partner. "I've got almost every cent I've saved invested in a shipment coming in by train from St. Louis tomorrow. That was our deal. My money and Farnell's wagons, mule-teams and knowhow. Equal shares in the profits."

"How does the deal stand with Farnell dead?" Clayburn asked softly.

"The same. Except that it's going to be harder without him."

"And the profits?"

She stiffened just a bit. "I was to get half. That hasn't

changed. Only now Farnell's share will be going to his family."

Clayburn was silent, his greenish eyes on her face.

She met his gaze directly. "That's one thing I never cheat on, Clayburn. I always pay what I owe."

The waiter brought their food. Over the meal she told Clayburn about how she'd met Harry Farnell in St. Louis. He'd gone there to try buying a big shipment on credit, without success. A mutual acquaintance, a big cattle buyer who didn't seem to mind having lost a considerable amount to her over the poker table, introduced them. Farnell loosened up with her more than he might have with a man. He'd told her of the plan he had for recouping his business losses, if he could only get his hands on a big shipment of supplies.

Farnell had just come from Bannock, up in the mountains some fifteen days riding northwest of Parrish. Shortly before he'd left there'd been a big gold strike there. Miners were pouring into Bannock by the hundreds—and the place was very short of supplies. It was already beginning to snow up there. In another few weeks, more or less, Bannock would be snowed in and it would no longer be possible to get freight wagons through to it.

Anybody getting there with supplies before the big snows blocked the way would make a fortune. Every item brought in would bring twenty times its worth—in gold.

With that kind of payoff as a reward, Farnell hadn't had to do much persuading to get Cora Sorel to sink her money into the venture as his partner. Outside of his cash shortage, he apparently had no troubles with anyone.

"He had trouble, all right," Clayburn said. "Trouble worth killing over."

"Not that he told me about."

"He could have been afraid to. Afraid you'd pull out of your deal with him."

"If so, he misjudged me. I've played in some risky games before. For smaller profits. I'd have stuck, no matter what."

Clayburn guessed that she would have. There was steel in her, under that soft, provocative exterior.

"Without Farnell, who're you planning to have take your freight wagons through to Bannock for you?"

"I'm taking them through myself. With men I'll hire to follow my orders."

"That's a rough trail for a woman," Clayburn told her. "First a stretch of desert. Then Bad Lands that won't be any picnic either; I've been up that way. And those mountains are usually crawling with Apache war parties."

"I know all about that. I'm going. Just as I intended to from the start."

"Even when Farnell was alive to take the wagons up?"

"That's right. Farnell seemed a decent enough sort. But I don't trust anyone that much. Those supplies are going to trade for an awful lot of gold. I intend to be there to keep count when the gold is paid over."

They were finishing the meal when a man entered the dining room, glanced around, and then walked straight toward their table. He was a stocky, well-dressed, cold-eyed man in his early forties, with thinning gray hair and a strong-featured, handsome face. Clayburn remembered seeing him among the first of the crowd that had gathered when the stage pulled into Parrish.

Behind him and a little to either side trailed two other men, not so well dressed. Clayburn had never seen either before, but he knew the look and the manner. They were acting as bodyguards. One was a massively built bruiser with huge hands and a face that looked as if it had been scrambled by several blows from a sledgehammer sometime in his past. The other was a slim, surly-faced kid who kept irritably brushing the fingertips of his right hand over his thigh as he moved, missing the feel of the gun he'd ordinarily be packing there.

The well-dressed man in the lead stopped at their table, his cold eyes flicking over Clayburn to settle on Cora Sorel. "Miss Sorel, I haven't had the pleasure of being introduced to you, so may I introduce myself? My name's Adler. George Adler."

Watching Cora Sorel's lack of expression as she sized Adler up, Clayburn saw part of the reason for her success as a gambler.

"How do you know who I am?" she asked, nothing in her voice but natural curiosity.

"You were pointed out to me earlier today."

"Pointed out?" Her eyebrows arched just a bit. "For what reason?"

"A pretty woman interests everyone." He smiled at her, but nothing warmed in the depths of his eyes. "I have a business offer for you," he went on smoothly. "May I sit down?"

"Of course. Business offers are something I'm always willing to listen to."

Adler took one of the other chairs, giving his full attention to her. But his bodyguards, standing and watching, kept their eyes on Clayburn.

"I was sorry to hear about the death of your partner," Adler told Cora Sorel. "I knew Harry Farnell slightly. Last met him up in Bannock, just before he left for St. Louis. As a matter of fact, it seems that both of us got the same idea after the gold strike. The idea of taking supplies into Bannock before the snows close the way. I also have a shipment coming in on the train tomorrow afternoon, this being the closest point on the railroad to Bannock. And I have wagons ready to carry the stuff."

Adler paused and hunched forward a little on his chair, his face earnest. "Miss Sorel, with Farnell dead and unable to take your wagons to Bannock, you're stuck with all those supplies you paid for. My offer is this: I'm prepared to take those supplies from you. I'll pay what you put out for them—plus a tidy profit."

Clayburn leaned back in his chair, forcing his shoulders to relax against the tension suddenly building up in him.

Cora Sorel asked thinly, "Parrish-type profit, Mr. Adler? Or Bannock-sized profit?"

Adler fashioned another smile for her. "We're in Parrish. It's right here I'd be buying. I'll pay you what the goods are worth here, and enough extra to make it worth while selling to me rather than any of the general stores in town.''

Cora Sorel smiled back at Adler. ''Those supplies will be worth twenty times that much in Bannock.''

Adler moved his hand impatiently as though brushing aside her statement. ''My offer is your only way out, financially. Unless you plan to hire some man to take Farnell's place in getting your freight to Bannock. And I advise you strongly against trusting anyone that far, with so much temptation.''

''I don't intend to, Mr. Adler. *I'm* taking my shipment to Bannock.''

Adler shook his head disapprovingly. A deep line of concentration dug itself in between his eyes. ''That's foolish—a lone woman, with the rough sort of men you'll need to handle the wagons, that far from civilization. It wouldn't be safe for you.''

''I own a gun,'' Cora Sorel told him coolly. ''And I know how to use it. I've taken care of myself in the uncivilized world for quite some time.''

''You worry me, Miss Sorel. . . .''

''I'll bet she does,'' Clayburn cut in softly. ''And so did Farnell.''

Adler's cold eyes fastened on him without expression. ''What do you mean by that?''

Clayburn's hard, cynical eyes stared back at Adler steadily. ''Two separate wagon trains getting to Bannock about the same time would cut into your profits. There'd be twice as many supplies, cutting down the worth of each item. And with the people there having a choice of who to buy from, you couldn't hold out for the kind of profits you'd like. You'll make even less if she gets to Bannock before you do. Her supplies would be all sold by the time you got there. Bannock's most pressing needs would already be satisfied. You'd have to sell to slightly less anxious buyers.''

''That's a consideration, of course,'' Adler admitted tightly. ''I didn't claim to be offering her charity.''

Clayburn's mouth twisted derisively. Mockery crept into

his voice. "What did you offer Farnell, up there in Bannock? Maybe you just warned him. Warned him that if he tried competing with you, you'd find a way to stop him."

The big bruiser took a step toward Clayburn. Adler stopped him with a quick gesture. He and Clayburn continued to stare at each other. Then Adler turned back to Cora Sorel.

"I made you a fair offer," he said, his manner now abrupt, the words coming out clipped and hard. "You'd be wise to accept it. As I told you, it's a long way to Bannock, through bad country. Anything could happen to you along the way." He had allowed a faint hint of threat to leak into his voice. Not much; just enough to be felt.

She continued to smile at him, unmoved. "Thanks for telling me. I like to know the rules before I sit in on a game."

"This is no game. It could be very dangerous for you—even fatal." Adler stood up. "Think it over carefully. You have time. Until the train arrives tomorrow afternoon. I won't repeat my offer. You can come to me anytime you decide to accept it. My room is in this hotel."

He turned and walked away without another glance at Clayburn.

But his two bodyguards went on looking at Clayburn for a moment before they followed Adler.

FOUR

Cora Sorel dropped her smile as she looked at Clayburn. "You think he's the one who paid them to kill Farnell."

"Smells that way." His greenish eyes watched her. "Any chance of your taking Adler's offer?"

"Not a chance in the world. If he wants to make it a race to Bannock, he'll get one."

"He'll do more than race you. He'll try to stop you."

She nodded, frowning. "He made that clear enough."

"You'll need a man to take Farnell's place as wagon captain. You want to go along all the way to Bannock to make sure you're not cheated, and I can see your point. But it'll take a man to run things on that trail, make no mistake about that."

She eyed him calculatingly. "Sounds almost like you want the job yourself."

"I do."

"Why?" Her voice was wary.

Clayburn's lips thinned. "There's a man I want to meet again. He's likely to show up wherever Adler needs another killing job done for him."

'That young redhead?"

"Uh-huh."

She thought about the story the marshal had told her of what Clayburn had done at the stage station; put that together with the way she read the look of him. She knew how to read men; she'd learned across a lot of poker tables. And in a number of situations that hadn't had anything to do with gambling.

But there were certain practical considerations.

"Being captain of a wagon train requires experience."

"I have it," he told her flatly. "Ran a few supply trains through to the posts in Arizona Territory when I was scouting for the army. Don't worry, I can handle the job."

Cora Sorel's dark eyes regarded him with some surprise. "Gambler, army scout, wagon captain . . . You've had a varied life. Anything else you've done?"

Clayburn shrugged. "This and that. I get restless."

She made up her mind. "All right. The job's yours."

"Good." Clayburn's long, lean fingers drummed softly on the table as he focused on the problems ahead. "How many wagons have you got?"

"Eight."

"How about men to drive them?"

"I've got six teamsters. Men who worked for Harry Farnell pretty regularly. All good men, according to him. In the morning you can help me hire the other two we'll need."

"If those two men Adler had with him are samples of his crew," Clayburn said, "it'll take more than muleskinners to get your wagons through. We'll need some men to ride guard. The right kind of men."

Cora Sorel nodded. "I've been giving that some thought."

"Anyone in mind?"

"Not yet."

"All right, then. I'll hunt around and see what I can find."

"Subject to my approval," she told him firmly.

"Fair enough."

They talked money. She didn't have much left, and the wages she could offer were not exceptional. But she compensated with the size of the bonus she was willing to pay each man after the freight was sold in Bannock.

"I'd like an advance on my wages," Clayburn said after they'd settled the matter.

Coral Sorel opened the handbag on her lap, counted fifty dollars onto the table. "Enough?"

"It'll do. Care to play some poker?"

An hour later, in her room on the top floor of the hotel, Clayburn pushed the last of the fifty dollars she'd advanced him across the table to her.

"You play mighty slick poker." Nothing in his face or voice betrayed that he'd discovered the tiny notches on the brand new cards, where she'd marked them with her thumb nail while dealing.

"I've had a lot of practice," she said with just a glint of humor in her dark eyes.

A corner of Clayburn's mouth quirked. "Looking good enough to eat helps, too. Takes a man's mind off the game." It had certainly taken his mind off it. Usually he sat down to poker in a naturally suspicious frame of mind. Only the heady effect of being alone in the softly lit bedroom with her had kept him from feeling those markings for so long.

She smiled at him. "I was told that, long ago, by a riverboat gambler. It's what started me on my career. Are you quitting?"

"Not if you'll advance me another fifty dollars on my wages."

Cora Sorel shrugged. "It's your money." She pushed over the fifty she'd won from him. "This makes it a hundred dollars' worth of wages I've advanced you."

Clayburn nodded. "At this rate you won't owe me anything but a good-by drink when we get to Bannock."

Fifteen minutes later he'd memorized all her thumbnail notches. After that his fingertips were able to read the cards she'd marked as he dealt them. By the time she realized that he was not just having a phenomenal run of luck, he'd won back his wages plus forty-two dollars of her money.

She eyed him suspiciously as he showed three aces to beat her three kings. He raked in the pot, smiling innocently.

Suddenly she gave a soft laugh. "Took you longer to catch on than I expected."

"You make it hard for a man to concentrate."

The way those greenish eyes of his looked at her began to have an effect that surprised her. Deliberately, she kept her tone light, "I couldn't resist trying, just to find out what you were made of. I did warn you there was only one thing I don't cheat about."

Clayburn nodded. "You warned me. Now I know you meant it."

Cora stood up. "Well, now that we know a little more about each other, I think I'll turn in for the night. I want to be fresh tomorrow."

His eyes followed her for a moment. She moved with a pantherish grace that accentuated her sensual looks. He got up and went to the window, closed the shutters and locked them.

She watched him, head cocked a little to one side. "Making yourself at home?"

"Just taking precautions. If it was Adler that had Farnell stopped, he could try stopping you next."

"Your concern is touching, but unnecessary. I do know how to take care of myself. You can feel quite safe about me. Or were you thinking of guarding me all night?"

His mouth quirked in a grin, but his eyes continued to look at her in a way that made her knees go weak. "I would feel safer about you if you weren't spending the night alone."

Slowly she shook her head. "That's just a bit too fast for me, Clay," she said softly, finding that it required an effort to keep her voice steady. "I don't know you *that* well."

Clayburn picked up his hat. "You will," he told her, and went out.

He waited in the corridor until he heard her lock the door from inside.

Wilks waited in the darkness of a cottonwood south of Parrish. He sat on the hard earth leaning back against the trunk of the tree, studying the stars overhead while his two horses nibbled at the sparse grass under the branches. The faint sounds of men approaching on foot brought him swiftly to his feet, his fingertips automatically brushing the grip of his holstered Colt.

The figures of three men appeared through the starlit darkness. George Adler, flanked by the broken-faced bruiser and the slim kid. When they were close enough Wilks noted that they wore no guns, at least none that showed. Adler hadn't wanted to attract attention to their slipping out of Parrish by claiming their guns from the marshal's office.

"Hello, Mr. Adler," Wilks greeted him. "Farnell get into Parrish all right?"

"He came in just fine, Wilks. Exactly the way I wanted him."

"He caught on soon as he saw me. Must've remembered seeing us together up in Bannock."

"I hear you had some trouble getting the job done."

Wilks laughed. "I didn't have any trouble at all. Ryle and Pollock did, though." He held out his left hand, palm up. "Pay-up time, Mr. Adler."

Adler drew the money from his pocket and handed it over. Wilks counted it, stuffed it in his own pocket. He didn't take his eyes from Adler. "That's just two hundred. You promised six hundred."

"Six hundred for the three of you," Adler said. "That comes to two hundred apiece. That's your third, like I agreed."

"Uh-uh. You said six hundred for doing the job. The job's been done. Ain't my fault Ryle and Pollock ain't around to share it with me." His voice had acquired a nasty cutting edge to it. He held out his left hand again. "Give."

The big bruiser on Adler's right shifted his feet.

Wilks snapped, "Don't get nervous, Benjy." His hand slapped lightly against his holster. The sound froze the big man.

Adler hadn't really expected to get away with it. Besides, he might be needing Wilks again. Getting the rest of the money from his other pocket, he placed it in Wilks' waiting palm. "I may have more work for you, on the trail to Bannock."

"I can always use more cash," Wilks said agreeably.

"Then hole up in the Sangre Blanco gorge and wait for me. I'll be bringing the freight up through there."

"I'll be there." Wilks pocketed the money and untethered his horses, watching Adler's bodyguards while he did so.

"Be careful," Adler told him. "Sheriff's out with a posse hunting you."

"They'll play hell tryin' to follow the trail I left." Wilks swung up onto his saddle, tugged the other horse by its lead rope, and rode off into the darkness.

Dillon, the thin, surly kid with Adler, said softly, "He don't look so tough to me. If I'd've had my gun, you wouldn't've had to pay him the rest of that dough."

"You've never seen Wilks in action," Adler told him shortly. "I have. You wouldn't stand a chance against him. Besides, I still need him."

"You figure the Sorel woman's still gonna try hauling freight up to Bannock herself?"

Adler nodded. "If I'm any judge, she's got that Clayburn fellow backing her all the way."

Dillon rubbed his thin hand on his thigh. "She wouldn't have him for long, if I could get hold of a gun in . . ."

"Shootin' ain't the only way to kill a man," Benjy cut in heavily.

Adler looked at the big, powerful man thoughtfully. "You must might have an idea there."

Benjy grinned, showing broken teeth. "Man's found beaten to death, ain't no way of provin' it didn't happen in a fair fight."

"It's worth trying," Adler said slowly. "Where's Slope?"

"Makin' a round of the saloons, like usual."

"Get him."

They walked back through the night to Parrish City.

* * *

Prowling the town, Clayburn found one of the biggest and rowdiest saloons in the red-light district and went in. He stuck to the crowded bar for a time, not drinking much, mostly looking and listening. With the probability of trail trouble from Adler's crew and Apaches, he knew exactly the kind of men he needed.

By the time he left the saloon he'd found the first of them—Ranse Blue, a scrawny, seedy, sour-faced man in his late fifties. Blue was working as the saloon's swamper, but he'd been a buffalo hunter until he'd been reduced to this a few years ago by the finishing off of the big wild herds. Which meant he'd be a superb rifle shot, injun-wary, and know how to hunt and read tracks.

Eagerness glowed in Ranse Blue's bloodshot eyes as Clayburn told him about the job. But the rest of his seamed, weather-ruined face remained sour. "What kind of pay you offerin'?" he demanded suspiciously.

When Clayburn told him, Blue's sourness increased. "That ain't much—for a man with all my experience."

Clayburn told him about the bonus, though he was quite certain the old buffalo hunter would have been willing to work for next to nothing at any job less humiliating than his present one. He understood that Blue's hesitation was merely pride-salving.

Blue pretended doubt as he considered the bonus offer. "Wouldn't get that unless we got to Bannock okay."

"We'll get there."

"Still a long time to wait. Now, if you was to offer me enough of an advance on that . . . Been a long time between drunks for me."

The owner of the saloon appeared at Ranse Blue's elbow, glaring. "What the hell're you loafing around the bar for, Ranse? You still ain't swept out the upstairs rooms."

Clayburn drew ten dollars from his pocket and put it on the bar in front of Ranse Blue. The old buffalo hunter studied the money briefly, glanced at his boss, then turned and yelled to the barkeep, "Whiskey, Mac! Half-bottle."

"Hold on," the saloon owner snapped. "You know you ain't allowed to do any drinking till after you finished work."

Ranse Blue grinned at him evilly. "I *am* finished. I just quit. Got me another job."

Clayburn walked away, left the saloon, and went hunting for more likely candidates.

He was passing a wide, deep-shadowed alley when a drunk came lurching up the boardwalk toward him. The drunk, wearing what looked like some prospector's cast-offs, was a man of medium height with short legs, a long torso and heavy, sloping shoulders. There was a long white scar between his upper lip and the base of his nose, like a mustache. He staggered head-down at Clayburn, who side-stepped closer to the mouth of the alley to avoid him.

The scar-faced drunk appeared to trip over his own feet. He sagged into a low crouch as though to keep from falling on his face. Then, abruptly, he ceased to be a drunk. He swiveled around and launched himself straight at Clayburn. The top of his head rammed into Clayburn's middle and knocked him backward into the wide alley.

Clayburn caught his balance quickly, his feet spreading slightly apart and his hands closing into fists. The scar-faced man straightened from his crouch and came after him. A thick, heavy arm snaked around Clayburn's neck from behind and dragged him deeper into the shadowed alley. A fist came from somewhere to his left and bounced off the side of his head. The scar-faced man surged in with both fists coming up for a clubbing blow at Clayburn's face.

Clayburn's right leg came up hard, the heel of his boot thudding into the scar-faced man's chest and slamming him against the wall. He brought his foot back down and stamped on the foot of the man holding him from behind. At the same time he twisted his body, jammed his elbow back into the man's gut, grabbed one of his fingers and tried to break it. There was a gasp of pain, the thick finger was wrenched from his grip, and Clayburn was freed. He twisted all the way around, striking out blindly. His fist sank deep into thick muscles and the man stumbled backward. Someone rammed all his weight low against the backs of Clayburn's legs. He hit the dirt face down, rolled fast. He was coming up on one knee when he saw who the other two men were by the faint light filtering down into the alley from a second-story window. They were Adler's bodyguards—the hulking bruiser and the lean, surly kid.

It was then that he realized they weren't just a bunch trying to knock him out and rob him. He yelled as loud as he could as he came up on his feet. All three of them landed on him, their weight driving him back down, a hand clamping over his mouth to cut the yell short. Clayburn sank his teeth into flesh. There was a cry and the hand whipped away. Clayburn started another shout. A fist smashed into his mouth. Blood flowed back into his throat. He struggled against the weight of their bodies, his knee jamming into someone's hip, his left hand closing on a throat. Fists pounded his body and face. Hands clutched at his arms, trying to hold them.

He managed to throw one man off, wrenched out of the grasp of another, fought his way up onto his knees. A boot kicked him in the temple. He sprawled on his back, consciousness ebbing for moment. They got his arms in that moment, one man on either side of him, pinning his arms to the ground. The hulking bruiser came down on Clayburn's stomach with both knees, knocking all the wind out of him. A fist like an anvil crashed down against Clayburn's head, triggering an explosion inside his brain.

"Hold him!" the bruiser on top of Clayburn panted. "Hold him. . . ."

He raised another big fist like a club and swung it full force at Clayburn's face. With the bruiser's weight pinning him down, and the other two men holding his arms and tangling his legs inside theirs, all Clayburn could do was twist his head away from the blow. He twisted it, but not far enough. Heavy knuckles caught him behind the ear. His head seemed to swell up like a balloon.

The fist went up again, came down.

And again.

Darkness swallowed him.

FIVE

Clayburn opened his eyes. The left one did not open all the way. But he could see out of both of them. Above him was a heavy-timbered ceiling. He gazed up at it thoughtfully. After a time he raised his hand and felt the area around his left eye. It was puffed, and very tender. His fingertips moved downward, traced the length of a strip of plaster on his cheek, and explored his nose. It was still in one piece. The fingertips went on to his mouth. His lips were swollen and torn. Some of the front teeth were loose, but none were missing. That surprised him. He let his hand fall back on the hard cot and wondered about it.

Finally he rolled his head and looked to his right. There were iron bars running from floor to ceiling where a wall would have been. He was in the Parrish jailhouse, in one of the two cells formed by the bars behind the office.

In the other cell a man was pacing back and forth as though trying to work off some of his excess energy. He looked like he had a lot to work off. He was very tall, more than a head taller than Clayburn, with a powerful, lanky build topped by the widest shoulders Clayburn had ever seen. His straight hair was pitch black, and his face might have been stolen from an Aztec statue carved out of dark granite.

For a while, Clayburn just lay there watching the giant Aztec pace the confined limits of his cell. Gradually, strength and feeling seeped back into him. With it came the awareness that his entire body hurt and his head ached horribly. The man in the other cell came to a halt at his locked door. His great hands seized the bars and for a second he seemed to be considering tearing them open. Instead, he shut his eyes, leaned his forehead against a bar, and stayed that way.

Clayburn turned his head toward the door to his own cell. It hung open. He tried to sit up, found that his abdomen muscles were too sore to help. Rolling on one side he got an arm under him, eased his legs off the cot, and forced himself to a sitting position. He got it done, but it tore a groan out of him.

The man in the next cell turned his face slightly and looked his way. Then he raised his head and shouted through the bars, "Hey, marshal! Your guest just woke up!"

He had a faint touch of Mexican accent.

The rear door of the office opened and Marshal Kavanaugh came through and into Clayburn's cell. He regarded Clayburn clinically. "How do you feel?"

"How do I look?"

The marshal shrugged. "I've seen worse."

"Then I guess I've felt worse. It's just that I can't remember when."

Marshal Kavanaugh's smile flickered on, and off. "Doctor looked you over. Couldn't find anything broken; no permanent damage. But I admit you don't look the man you used to."

Clayburn leaned back against the wall, exhausted by the effort of sitting. "How'd I get here?"

"Your friends carried you."

"Friends?"

"The three that were beating up on you."

Clayburn's eyes were dull. But in their depths something smoldered. "Nice of them," he whispered.

"Not very. I was walking behind them all the way, with my hand on my gun."

"You always manage to be in the right place at the right time?"

Kavanaugh shrugged. "Sooner or later. Man passing by

heard yelling in the alley, looked in and came running for me. I went over and called 'em off you. They said it was just a little fist fight, but I didn't like the odds. Three of them and you unconscious."

Clayburn looked at the other cell. "Where're you holding them?"

"I'm not. Hell, if I locked somebody up every time a man took a beating in this town, I'd need ten more cells. If it'd happened in the respectable section of town I'd fine 'em for disturbing the peace, but . . ."

"All right," Clayburn cut in wearily. "I get the point. They say anything about why they jumped me?"

"According to them, Slope was staggering drunk, bumped into you by accident and you played it tough, started to rough Slope up. So Benjy and Dillon jumped in to help him out."

"Slope the one with the scar?"

"Uh-huh."

"He wasn't drunk."

"Benjy—that's the big fellow—and Dillon, they say he was too drunk to defend himself against you. You can bring charges against 'em if you want, but it's your word against theirs, and to tell you the truth . . ."

"Forget it." Clayburn shut his eyes against a wave of dizziness. He got hold of himself angrily, forcing his eyes open. They had a dazed, unfocused look. "Keep watch on Cora Sorel's room tonight," he said thickly, "or you may have worse than a beating on your hands. Those three work for a man named George Adler. He pressured her to sell her freight to him. She wouldn't, and she hired me as her wagon captain."

"You saying that's why they jumped you?"

"That's why." Clayburn had to concentrate to form each word. "If you hadn't warned me about making charges without proof, I'd bring up the subject of Farnell's murder, too. So keep an eye on her."

The marshal scowled over it. Finally he nodded. "Okay. I can spare a deputy for it. It's a quiet night, the way nights go here in Parrish."

"That's fine," Clayburn mumbled, and closed his eyes and let himself slide down the wall. He was asleep when his head touched the hard mattress.

When he opened his eyes again daylight was streaming in through the small barred window of his cell. He felt slept out and his nervous system seemed to be functioning normally once more. Raising a hand to rub the last of sleepiness from his face, he winced at the tenderness around his left eye.

"Good morning," a voice said.

Turning his head, he saw it was the giant Mexican with the Aztec face. He was now sitting on the edge of the other bunk in Clayburn's cell. Puzzled, Clayburn raised up on his elbow and looked at the other cell. Both bunks there were occupied by sleeping men and three more were curled up on the stone floor.

The Mexican glanced over his shoulder. "Got too crowded in there. Two of 'em got caught breaking into a general store. One's just a cowhand that got liquored up and made a pass at a respectable woman over in the residential section. The other two're his buddies that tried to stop the marshal from locking him up. Had to be pistol-whipped and carried in."

The Mexican turned his expressionless dark face back to Clayburn. "So the marshal moved me in here with you. Hope you don't mind. My name's Kosta."

"Don't mind at all." Clayburn shoved his legs off the bunk and sat up, leaning forward with his elbows on his knees to ease the stiff soreness in his midsection.

"Feeling better?" Kosta asked him.

"I'll do." Clayburn looked toward his cell door. It was still open. "Seems like the marshal trusts you."

"I promised to stay put," Kosta said, as if that were explanation enough.

"What're you in for?"

"Breaking up a saloon," Kosta told him, gently and regretfully. "And some arms and legs and noses." He smiled apologetically. "I was drunk, you see? Or I'd never have done anything like that. The marshal could tell you that. He knows I'm no trouble-maker. But I was drunk, and some man made a remark about Mexicans."

Kosta thought back on it. "I don't remember who said it, or what it was he said, to tell you the truth. But they say I threw him across the saloon and smashed the back-bar mirror with him. Then it seems all these friends of his jumped me." He shook his head sadly. "I did a lot of damage. Breakage and doctor bills and my fine came to three hundred and twenty dollars. I'd spent every cent I had on the liquor and couldn't pay it, so they sentenced me to thirty-two days—one day for every ten dollars."

Clayburn eyed him calculatingly. "You go on tears like that very often?"

"I sure don't. Last time I did anything like that was more'n two years ago. And I ain't likely to do it again. I'm going crazy, shut up in here like this."

The rear door of the marshal's office opened. A deputy came into their cell carrying a pot of steaming coffee and a tray with cups and fat rolls on it. He was a compact, wiry blond in his middle twenties, with a cheerfully ugly, pug-nosed face. "Fresh rolls," he announced as he sat down beside Kosta. "Bakery round the corner just fished 'em out of the oven." He set the tray on the floor between the bunks and grinned at Clayburn. "You look pretty fit for a man's just took a bad licking. My name's Jim Roud. I'm in charge around here for the marshal, daytimes. So anything you need . . ."

"All I need's some of that coffee."

"Don't we all." Deputy Roud began pouring into the three cups.

One of the men in the other cell sat up and whined, "Hey—how about some of that over here?"

"Shut up and wait!" Roud answered without looking around at the man. "Regular breakfast don't come in for another half hour."

Clayburn raised his cup to his lips. The coffee scalded going down, but he gulped all of it greedily and refilled his cup before picking up one of the warm rolls. As he ate it and sipped at his second cup, he studied Kosta.

"Ever handled mule teams, by any chance?"

The Mexican shook his head, swallowed the chunk of roll he'd been chewing. "Only horses. I've been a blacksmith. But mostly I'm a cook."

"Best in town," Roud said. "Before you pulled that one-man riot." The deputy looked to Clayburn. "Took five of us to bring him down. He nearly tore my arm off, doing it."

"I don't remember it," Kosta murmured. "You know I wouldn't do a thing like that sober."

"Done any trail cooking?" Clayburn asked.

"Sure. For some of the cattle outfits."

"Any good with a rifle?"

Kosta shrugged a massive shoulder. "Like most everybody. Why?"

"I'm running a string of freight wagons up to Bannock. We still need a couple drivers and guards—and a cook." Clayburn glanced at the deputy. "How many more days has he got to serve?"

"Fifteen."

"At ten dollars a day that means he still owes the town a hundred and fifty dollars, right?"

Jim Roud nodded.

Clayburn turned back to Kosta. "I might be able to persuade my boss to pay the rest of your fine for you—as an advance on wages. If you're interested."

Kosta looked at him as though he were his long-lost father. "Interested? I'd crawl all the way to Bannock for a chance to get out of here."

"We're expecting trouble all along the way," Clayburn warned.

"What kind?"

"Snow—if the blizzards hit before we reach Bannock, we could get stuck in the mountains and freeze to death. Apaches—we'll be cutting through hostile territory. And another outfit that's gonna try to stop us from reaching Bannock, or at least to keep us from getting there first."

He touched a long finger to the plaster stuck on his cheek. "They play rough."

"You don't know what rough is," Kosta rumbled, "till you been stuck in a little cell long as I have. Get me out of here and you've got a cook. And I *can* handle a rifle. Damn good."

Jim Roud was looking thoughtful. "Those guards you were saying you needed. . . . What kind of wages you paying?"

Clayburn told him about the wages and bonus arrangement. "Why? You know somebody good that'd be interested?"

"Yeah." Roud's ugly face creased in a smile. "Me."

Clayburn eyed the deputy over the rim of his cup. "Tired of being a lawman?"

"Kind of. This town life's beginning to bore me. Been a cowhand most of my life. Was, till Kavanaugh talked me into signing on as his deputy. Sounded like action so I took it on. But he's got this town so tamed there's hardly any excitement any more."

"You'll get all you want with us," Clayburn told him. As far as he was concerned, any man good enough to work for Kavanaugh was good enough for him. Cora Sorel had estimated that she could afford, besides Clayburn, three extra men to act solely as guards. The old buffalo hunter and Jim Roud made two.

"You're hired," he told Roud. "Any other of Kavanaugh's deputies itching for action and open spaces?"

"I'll ask around."

But when Clayburn met Cora Sorel an hour later, he found that the other guard had already been hired.

Cora Sorel was coming down off the porch of the hotel when Clayburn got there. This morning she was dressed in a trail outfit—a split riding skirt, boots, sheepskin jacket and a flat, wide-brimmed hat. It was quite a change from what she'd worn the night before, but she still looked good to Clayburn.

The man with her didn't.

He was about Clayburn's height and age, but much

slimmer, with long, delicate hands. There was a withdrawn, deadly quality to the man, something that emanated from the almost womanish grace with which he moved, the contemptuous set of his thin mouth, the empty expression of his thin face and eyes like dirty ice.

Clayburn knew the breed and disliked it instinctively. A killer. He couldn't be anything else.

SIX

Cora stared with shock at Clayburn's face. "What happened to you?"

"Three of Adler's crew happened to me." He told her about it briefly.

"Are you all right now? Will you still be able to . . ."

"I'm fine," he told her flatly, looking at the man with her.

Cora introduced them. The man's name was Matt Haycox. They eyed each other and nodded slightly, neither man offering his hand.

"Matt and I know each other from before," Cora told Clayburn. "He kept order in a gambling house in Butte." She gave Haycox an admiring look that seemed to Clayburn to be contrived for effect. "And he certainly did keep order. I've hired him."

"To do what?" Clayburn asked tonelessly.

Haycox smiled faintly, but his eyes remained empty. "To keep order," he said in a voice as dead as his face.

"As one of our guards," Cora added. "He can handle a gun better than any other man I ever saw."

Clayburn held down his irritation. "Has she told you I'm wagon captain?" he asked Haycox. "That means you'll have to take orders from me."

"She told me," Haycox drawled.

"All right, then take yourself a walk. Miss Sorel and I have things to talk over."

Haycox's thin mouth grew thinner. He looked to Cora.

She put her hand on his arm. "You go ahead, Matt. I'll see you at Farnell's freight office at noon."

Haycox's eyes slid back to Clayburn, held for a moment. Then he drifted away.

Cora turned to Clayburn. "You deliberately tried to offend him. Why?"

"I don't like him," Clayburn said simply.

"Be careful, Clay. He's a dangerous man to toy with."

"And maybe too dangerous to depend on."

Cora shook her head. "He's exactly what we need. And don't worry, I can handle him." She smiled. "He had a yen for me. I think he still does."

"I thought you were going to let me hire the guards," Clayburn said stonily.

"Subject to my approval," she reminded him. "Any men you hire are bound to consider themselves *your* men. I want one along who'll be *my* man—all the way. Matt Haycox fits that."

Clayburn's face softened. "I shouldn't have shown you so much of myself in that poker game last night. Now you don't trust me."

"I told you before, I don't trust *anybody* all the way." She put her hand on his arm exactly as she'd done with Haycox, and her eyes were warm on his. "It's nothing personal, Clay. Just a leftover of some unpleasant experiences in the past."

She was, Clayburn reflected, as used to gentling men as a mustanger was to gentling horses.

As they walked together toward the freight office down by the railroad tracks, Cora asked him, "Have you managed to find any other men for us?" She glanced at his bruised face. "Or weren't you in any shape to?"

Clayburn told her about the three men he'd turned up.

She liked the sound of Jim Roud and Kosta, but was leery about Ranse Blue. "He sounds too old for the kind of trip we're likely to have."

"He'll stand up to it as well as any of us. Blue's one of those that toughen with age. And he's spent years dodging hostiles in open country. Just the kind of man we'll need.

Somebody that can keep an eye on what Adler's outfit is up to without being spotted."

Cora Sorel finally accepted his choice, though reluctantly.

Behind the small adobe building housing Farnell's freighting office there was a warehouse for freight storage, an adobe-walled yard holding the wagons, and a corral in which the mules and horses were kept. Eleven men were gathered waiting in the yard between the big Murphy wagons. Six were the freighters who'd worked steadily for Farnell in the past—the kind of rough, violent-looking men you usually found in jobs like that. Men who could be hard to handle on occasion, but would be just as hard to scare.

The other five had showed up hoping for a job.

Cora Sorel let Clayburn do the talking. He told all of them what they faced, holding nothing back—the kind of country they'd have to cross, the blizzards in the mountains, the Apaches, the likelihood of interference from Adler's outfit. The six regulars heard him out with a stoic boredom, not budging, but one of the other five shrugged and walked away, looking sheepish.

Clayburn questioned the remaining four, rejected one because he'd never handled mule teams before, another because he appeared nervous and didn't ask about the pay. Clayburn had a hunch Adler had sent him.

If the two Clayburn hired—O'Hara and Fischman—had nerves they didn't show them. Both were big, solid men; the former was ex-army and the latter had once ridden shotgun for the Butterfield Stage. Both were well acquainted with mules.

Clayburn went over the wagons with the eight of them. There were fifteen wagons, reminders of the time before Farnell had gone bust, when he'd sometimes run as many as twenty in one train. But some of them were now badly in need of repair. They selected the eight in best condition. Leaving the teamsters to prepare the wagons and select their mule teams, he returned to the office and got from Cora a hundred-and-fifty dollar advance on Kosta's wages. Then he left to bail out Kosta and collect Jim Roud and Ranse Blue.

As he went up the street he met Haycox strolling toward the office.

They passed each other without speaking.

Marshal Kavanaugh made no fuss about losing his deputy. "Roud's been acting so itchy lately," he told Clayburn, "he'd've been sure to've got himself in trouble before long. And I'd have to bring him in and lock him up, badge or no badge. But you let him ride some of the wildness out of himself and you'll have a pretty good man on your hands."

And he was more than pleased to be able to release Kosta, though sorry that Parrish was losing a good cook.

Leaving the jail, Clayburn sent Kosta to the Farnell Freight Company headquarters to get his chuck wagon ready. He took ex-deputy Jim Roud along with him to hunt up the old buffalo hunter. It took them almost an hour before they found Ranse Blue, sprawled out in a drunken sleep behind a stable at the other end of town.

It took another half hour, and a dunking in a dirty horse trough, to get Blue awake and on his feet. Even then he couldn't stand without leaning on Roud. He had a horrible hangover and he looked even older than the night before—old and feeble and useless. The way he was, Clayburn knew Cora Sorel would balk at taking him on. And he'd need Blue, maybe more than any of the rest of them. So there was only one thing for it.

With Roud and Clayburn supporting him, they got Blue to the nearest saloon and bought him a double whiskey in a tumbler. Clayburn watched the old man gulp it, hanging onto the bar with his other hand. Drops of liquor trickled down his gray-whiskered chin, but he got most of it in, his scrawny figure shuddering violently as it went down.

When the shuddering stopped, Blue straightened a bit and turned his bloodshot, red-rimmed eyes on Clayburn. "Another one of those," he croaked, "and I can maybe let go of this bar."

Clayburn bought him another double. Blue swallowed it like water, this time without a shudder. He set the empty glass down, sighed weakly, and then took his hand off the bar and straightened all the way. "See?" He wiped a hand over his wrinkled face and, surprisingly, some of his years seemed to drop away from him. He even managed a one-sided grin. "Good as new."

"Are you going to need whiskey along the trail to keep you going?" Clayburn demanded.

"Hell no. I only drink in towns. Never take any liquor along with me on the trail."

"That better be a fact. Because part of our freight'll be a wagonload of liquor. I catch you breaking into that and I'll boot you out of the outfit without a horse—no matter where we are at the time."

"I said I don't drink on the trail," Blue snarled. "I just needed one big drunk to kiss this lousy town good-by is all. You don't believe me, t'hell with you."

The strength of Blue's anger reassured Clayburn some. He was turning from the bar when he became aware of the sounds of wagons. Crossing the room, he looked out over the batwings at the street—in time to see George Adler ride by wearing a rough trail outfit. From the way he sat his horse he was obviously no city man, and there was something formidable about Adler that hadn't shown the night before. His wide face was no longer concealing anything, and ruthlessness was written plain on it.

The bearlike Benjy and the surly kid named Dillon rode on either side of their boss. Behind them rattled Adler's empty wagons, drawn by their teams of mules, following Adler down toward the railroad tracks to be ready when the train pulled in. Since Farnell's Freight Company sided the tracks, there was no such need to get Cora Sorel's wagons lined up for the arrival of the train. There was a ramp leading directly from the tracks into the warehouse, up which they could carry the supplies and roll the barrels of flour, sugar and other foodstuffs Cora had bought for Bannock, as they were off-loaded from the freight cars.

The loading of Cora's wagons would take place inside Farnell's freight yard.

Clayburn counted Adler's wagons as they rolled past. There were twelve of them, each handled by a hardcase teamster. Riding behind the last wagon came the scar-faced man called Slope, and four other men Clayburn pegged as gunfighters.

Clayburn's eyes were narrowed as he gazed after them.

Behind him, Jim Roud asked quietly, "That the outfit we're expecting to tangle with?"

"That's them," Clayburn said, half to himself. Adler's crew outnumbered his own by seven men. Bad odds, but not quite as bad as he'd expected.

It might, he decided, be as good a time as any to find out what his own crew was made of.

Striding back to the bar, he purchased two full bottles of whiskey. Carrying a bottle in each hand, he headed for Farnell's Freight Company, flanked by Roud and Blue.

Some thirty minutes later, with the wagons ready and nothing left to do but wait for the train, Clayburn gathered Cora Sorel and the men inside the one-room warehouse next to the freight ramp.

"I figure it's time for our last drink between here and Bannock," he told them, and looked at Cora. "If that's all right with you?"

Cora made an open gesture with her graceful, slim-fingered hands. "You're running this game from here on, Clay. I'm only the boss."

"Well then . . ." Clayburn picked up one of the whiskey bottles and uncorked it. He handed it solemnly to Cora. "You first—boss."

She hesitated, until she saw the amused way in which he was watching to see what she'd do. Then she raised the bottle, her warm smile taking in the other men, and made a toast: "Here's to Bannock, to a big profit for me and a big bonus for each of you . . . . and to hell with George Adler."

She tipped the bottle to her lips and took a swallow. She

even managed to do it without wincing. Clayburn admired her control.

Lowering the bottle, Cora passed it to her pet killer, Matt Haycox, who was near her like a watchdog.

"I don't drink," Haycox said quietly, and passed the bottle on to the next man.

No one else voiced a similar quirk. By the time the bottle had gone halfway around, it was empty. Clayburn uncorked the other bottle and tossed it to the next man in line. When it reached Ranse Blue, the last man before Clayburn, there was about the equivalent of three doubles left in the bottom.

Clayburn snagged the bottle out of Blue's hands before it reached his lips. "You don't drink either," he informed Blue, and tilted the bottle to his own mouth, keeping it that way until he'd swallowed the last drop.

He lowered the bottle with a gasp, tossed it aside, and grinned at his crew. His eyes were suddenly very bright. There was a wildness in them that Cora Sorel hadn't noticed before.

"Let's go have a look at the opposition," he said, and strolled out onto the loading ramp.

The others crowded out after him and looked at Adler's wagons and men lined up along the opposite side of the tracks. Clayburn's eyes sought out Adler, held on him for a second, and then moved on to the hulking bruiser next to him.

"Hello, Benjy."

Benjy scowled at him, puzzled by the lack of animosity in Clayburn's tone.

Clayburn started down the ramp toward him, his pace leisurely, his mouth smiling. His hands hung straight down at his sides, his long fingers flexing.

But Benjy was not looking at his hands. He was studying his face. And as Clayburn reached the tracks, Benjy's scowl became a sneer.

"What happened to you, Clayburn? You look kind of beat up."

"I *was* beat up," Clayburn said, and by the time he'd said it he was across the tracks and Benjy was within reach.

Without preamble, he drove his right fist into Benjy's stomach.

SEVEN

Benjy sagged backward, clutching his middle, his face contorted as he fought for breath. Adler hastily got out of the way as Dillon leaped at Clayburn with fists swinging.

Clayburn swiveled slightly at the hips, not shifting his feet, and backhanded Dillon across the face. The blow twisted Dillon's head around and flung him against a wagon. As he bounced off it, Clayburn hit him with his other hand as hard as he could. Dillon's eyes went blank. He hit the dirt on his side and stayed that way.

It had given Benjy a chance to catch his breath, though he still couldn't straighten up fully. He came at Clayburn with murder in his face. Clayburn turned to meet his rush, sensing the rest of Adler's bunch converging on them, hoping his own crew was moving in behind him.

Clayburn was in no mood for boxing with the bigger man. There was a wildness flaming inside him, demanding vengeance for what had happened in that dark alley. He met Benjy head-on, took a chest blow that threatened to break a rib, and smashed a left and right to Benjy's face with all the power of his shoulders and back. Benjy stumbled sideways and spat out the stump of a tooth. Clayburn went after him and aimed a right at the big man's nose. Benjy ducked. Clayburn's fist rammed into his forehead. It was like hitting a boulder. Clayburn's arm went numb all the way to his shoulder and for a second he thought his knuckles were broken. The punch didn't seem to affect Benjy at all. He bored in for the kill.

Hard knuckles skidded off Clayburn's cheek, ripping away the plaster over the previous cut. A fist slammed into his heart, knocking him backward and spinning him around. Benjy leaped at his back, but didn't get there on time. Clayburn caught his balance, wrenched himself around to face Benjy, and drove his left forearm into the big man's throat.

Benjy teetered on his heels, gagging, eyes bulging in their sockets. Clayburn spread his feet and began driving one punch after another into the other man. Having learned his lesson, he kept away from Benjy's head, concentrating on sinking short, chopping blows into the midsection. Benjy fought back with all his superior weight and strength. But the impact of the first blows had taken some of the steam out of him. He couldn't stand up against Clayburn's cold, relentless fury. He began backing away, legs buckling, eyes glazing.

The sight of Benjy being broken was too much for Adler's crew. The nearest ones closed in. A man grabbed Clayburn's right wrist with both hands and hung on. Another landed on his back, wrapping an arm around his throat. Slope suddenly appeared between Clayburn and Benjy, launching a kick at Clayburn's stomach.

Clayburn knocked Slope's kick aside with his knee, tried to punch with his free fist at the man hanging onto his arm. But the man on his back abruptly increased the pressure of his arm against Clayburn's throat, strangling him and dragging his head back. Blood pounded against the backs of Clayburn's eyes, blurring his vision. The weight of the two men bore him to the ground on his knees. Slope stepped in fast to drive a bootheel against Clayburn's face.

Slope's foot was coming up off the ground when Jim Roud materialized out of nowhere and rammed into him bodily. The two men tumbled to the ground, Roud on top with both fists swinging.

A split-second later the weight was plucked from Clayburn's back.

He caught a blurred glimpse of the towering Kosta, his dark face a mask of fury, the man struggling uselessly in the grip of his enormous hands. Kosta raised the man high in the air and threw him headfirst against a wagon wheel. Then he turned, reached down for the man hanging onto Clayburn's arm, and lifted him away as though he were a puppy.

By then the whole area had exploded into a free-for-all between the two wagon crews.

Clayburn came to his feet and found himself hemmed in by a knot of surging, stamping, fist-flailing men. He broke free of the crush, tripped over a falling man, knocked aside another man. Then he and Benjy found each other.

Benjy had had time to recover. He knocked aside Clayburn's fist and rammed a punch into Clayburn's jaw. Clayburn took it, shook his head once, hard, and struck back. For a few seconds they slugged it out toe to toe. Then the driving power behind Clayburn's fists began to sap Benjy's strength again. And his courage. His punches became slow, wild. And then he backed off.

Before Clayburn could go after him, two wrestling teamsters fell against his back, knocking him off his feet. He landed on his hands and knees. Benjy lurched forward and kicked. The toe of his boot caught Clayburn's side and flopped him over on his back. Clenching his teeth against the pain of it, Clayburn saw Benjy's next kick coming straight at his head.

He rolled fast. The bootheel slashed past his ear. He grabbed the boot with both hands and twisted. Benjy sprawled face down in the dirt. Shoving to his feet, still holding onto the boot, Clayburn increased his pressure. Benjy's other boot hammered into his chest, hurling him away.

He staggered but stayed on his feet, bending forward and sucking air into his lungs, his heart thudding, waiting as Benjy came up off the ground.

The press of battling men around them suddenly shoved them against each other. And Benjy changed tactics. His fingers clawed for Clayburn's eyes; his knee came up at Clayburn's groin. Clayburn jerked his face away from the reaching fingers and he twisted, taking the knee on his hip. If Benjy wanted to fight the rest of it dirty, he was more than willing to oblige.

He grabbed both of Benjy's ears and yanked in opposite directions. Benjy screamed and tore himself loose. It left him wide open. Clayburn hit him well below the belt with a left, and then a right—measured, bludgeoning punches that bent him forward and down. Clayburn's knee came up to meet Benjy's nose, breaking it.

Benjy staggered back, blood streaming down over his mouth and chin. But he was a hard man to finish. He didn't go down. Clayburn closed in to put him down. Benjy hit him twice but there wasn't enough in either blow to stop him. He clubbed the side of Benjy's jaw. Benjy's legs bent, but his fingers groped for his enemy's throat. Clayburn waited till the hands were around his neck, leaned against them, and hooked a left deep into Benjy's middle. The hands dropped from his throat.

He clubbed Benjy's jaw again. And again . . . It was like chopping down a heavy tree with a blunt ax. It took time. But he got it done.

When the man lay face down at his feet, Clayburn took a moment to survey what was happening around him and see where else he was needed.

It appeared that he wasn't needed anywhere. He'd wanted to find out what his crew was made of. Now he knew. Jim Roud was getting up off Slope's unconscious form when one of Adler's gunmen slugged him in the ear and knocked him back down. Roud's feet shot out and kicked the other man's ankles out from under him. The next second the two of them were fighting it out in the dirt. Ranse Blue was engaged in teaching a man about twenty years younger than him a variety of vicious tricks he'd learned in battles with trappers and riverboat men—including eye-gouging, nose-biting and throat-kicking. Kosta was using one of Adler's men as a battering ram against three others.

And despite the odds Farnell's regular teamsters and the

two new recruits were holding their own against Adler's in as savage a mass brawl as Clayburn had ever witnessed.

Only three people held off from the fight, taking no part in it: Adler, Cora Sorel—and Matt Haycox. Cora's pet killer was where he usually was: at her elbow up on the ramp, showing no interest in what was happening.

At that moment Clayburn caught sight of one of his new teamsters, O'Hara, going limp under two of Adler's men. Instead of letting up, they went on pounding at his unconscious form.

Clayburn reached them in three long, fast steps. With his next stride, not slowing his momentum, he kicked one of Adler's men in the head. The man fell off O'Hara as though his neck were broken. Clayburn was turning to deal with the other one when the roar of shots froze him.

They froze everyone. Heads turned in the direction of the gunfire. Marshal Kavanaugh stood in the middle of the tracks pointing a Colt at the sky. Several yards to either side of him stood two deputies, holding sawed-off shotguns.

The marshal lowered his gun slowly, pointing it at no one and everyone. "Fun's fun," he said without heat. "Now you've all had yours and it's over. Next man that swings at anybody, I'll break his elbow or knee with a bullet."

"He's the one who started it," Adler stated, stabbing a finger at Clayburn. "For no reason. Just walked over and started hitting Benjy without warning."

Kavanaugh eyed Clayburn, who raised and lowered his shoulders in a slow shrug.

"Just a little fist fight, marshal. Same as last night. Only this time nobody was holding my arms. Not for long."

Marshal Kavanaugh sighed. "I don't know what it's about and I don't care. As of now. But if there's any more trouble between these two outfits, no matter who starts it, I'm gonna hold all of you in town while I try to find out. I figure the questioning might delay your departure as much as a week."

He paused to let the threat sink in. "Okay, Clayburn . . . get your men back on your own side of the tracks."

Clayburn did so. Some of the men needed help, but they left a number of Adler's men still sleeping it off beside the tracks.

An angry Cora met him on the ramp. "Just what was the point of that, Clay?"

He wiped blood from his mouth. "Just wanted to make sure all our crew are really on our side."

"That was a hell of a way to find out. Some of them will be in no condition to do their jobs for a couple of days."

"If they can't, they don't belong in our crew," Clayburn said. But he was no longer looking at her. His eyes were on Matt Haycox. "Are you part of this outfit, Haycox?"

Haycox stared back at him without expression. "You heard Cora say she hired me."

"I didn't see you earning your wages."

Haycox looked bored. "I'm being paid for my guns, not my fists. My hands are delicate, and useful. If I broke a knuckle on somebody's jaw, I wouldn't be much use to Cora."

He had a point. Clayburn had known other gunfighters who'd pampered their hands like musicians. That didn't change anything. Their dislike of each other ran deeper than logic. He was itching for a clash that would leave Haycox behind.

But whatever might have happened between them at that point was pushed aside by the sound of a distant train whistle.

Adler's outfit headed out of Parrish as soon as his wagons were loaded, pausing only long enough for his men to pick up their weapons from the marshal's office. Cora Sorel was in a fever to hurry after them.

Clayburn cooled her impatience. "We'll finish loading slow and careful. And get the doc to patch up any of our men that need it. Only a few hours to sunset. We'll camp just outside town. Tomorrow morning's when we make our start. I want distance between us and Adler.''

''Distance? From what Farnell told me, there's only a few trails through those mountains to Bannock. If Adler reaches the mountains first, he could block our route, force us to backtrack and . . .''

''Sure,'' he agreed amiably. ''If he gets there first.'' He smiled at her gently. ''But he won't.''

His certainty puzzled Cora. She wanted to argue with him, but something—something about the man himself that she couldn't put her finger on—stopped her. For the second time that day, she found herself reluctantly accepting his judgment over her own.

It was an hour before dusk when Cora Sorel's wagon train pulled out of Parrish. When they stopped at the jailhouse to collect their weapons, the marshal took Clayburn aside for a moment.

''It still ain't any of my business,'' he said, ''but if you're interested in a piece of advice . . .''

''From you . . . any time.''

''You need more men.''

''I know. But we've already got as many as the boss can pay.''

Kavanaugh scowled at him. ''That's too bad. Because Adler hired a couple extra before he headed out. Neither of 'em exactly the mule-skinner type.''

Clayburn nodded carelessly. ''Well—that figured to happen. Thanks for letting me know.''

''It doesn't worry you any?''

''It does. But then, I worry about most everything. I feel more comfortable that way.''

''Comfortable?''

''And safer. It's only the things you *don't* worry about that can hit you when you're not looking.''

He shook the marshal's hand and went back out to the wagons.

''All right . . . Roll 'em!''

EIGHT

They ate early and they ate well. Kosta proved to be as good a cook as he'd been said to be. By the first faint light of dawn Clayburn had Cora's wagon train on the move, proceeding northwest into rough desert country.

Kosta's chuck wagon, pulled by two teams of horses, moved out in the lead, followed by the eight mule-drawn freight wagons. Like each of the teamsters, Kosta had a gun strapped to his hip, a rifle close to hand, and extra ammunition for both behind the seat. Roud and Haycox rode off to either side of the wagon train as flankers, one or the other of them occasionally dropping back past the last wagon for a look over the horizon behind them. Cora Sorel, riding a fleet-footed buckskin with the sure grace of someone born to the saddle, acted as an extra flanker. She carried a Winchester in her saddle scabbard and a Colt .44 on her hip, and before many days had passed it was evident she was as equal to hard traveling as any of the men.

Ranse Blue was gone before they set out that first day, riding off into the predawn darkness, leading an extra horse so he could alternate mounts for speed if necessary. No one saw much of him in the days that followed. Clayburn had given the old buffalo hunter the job of spying on Adler's outfit. About every other night Blue would reappear, have himself a hot meal, fill his canteens and food bag, report to Clayburn, and be gone again well before dawn.

Clayburn rode point, well in advance of the wagons,

scouting the way. From time to time he'd ride a full circle around the wagon train, out of sight of it, scanning the distances through his army-issue field glasses. He returned to the wagons only for the midday halts and when they made camp for the night. He chose and arranged each campsite with an eye to defense, corralling the horses and mules securely within a box formed by the wagons, assigning guard duties so that there were always at least three out in the dark beyond the campfire light, watching and listening for the first signs of an attack.

Not that he was expecting trouble this early. But it was well to get everyone in the habit of being set for it from the start. Because he'd been looking for them, Clayburn had soon found tracks which indicated that riders from Adler's outfit were keeping tabs on Cora's wagon train, just as Blue was on Adler's.

Blue's first reports back were what Clayburn had anticipated. Adler was following a longer route across the desert country—a route determined by the known watering places along the way. Clayburn had chosen a more direct, much shorter route—but one that had to cross a couple of problems. The first problem was a three-day stretch across country that wasn't supposed to contain any water. The second problem was a long east-to-west expanse of rolling sand dunes in which the legs of the mules and wheels of the wagons might become too deep mired to get through.

They hit the three-day dry stretch a week out of Parrish. In readiness for it, Clayburn had had a huge cask of water secured on top of each wagon load. The mules and horses drank every last drop of it their first night into the dry stretch, but Clayburn did not appear anxious about it. He led the wagon train, an hour before dusk of the following day, to what everyone knew to be a dry lake.

It was a place where there'd once been water, fed by some underground spring which had suddenly stopped flowing several years back.

But the lake was no longer dry, as Clayburn had discovered a week and a half earlier while riding south, the day before his horse had broken a leg. As mysteriously as the underground spring had shut itself off, it had suddenly turned itself on again. The lake was half full of water.

Since leaving Parrish, Cora had taken her evening meals with Clayburn. Their growing ease with each other appeared to irritate Haycox, who was usually hovering nearby. That evening as they sat together after the mules and horses had been watered, she looked more cheerful than she had been the night before.

"You knew that lake had refilled all along, Clay. Why didn't you say so?"

He smiled at her. "It might've emptied itself again since I last saw it."

"Then what would we have done?"

"Gone two days without water. It would have been hard on the mules—but we'd have made it."

"And I suppose you've also known all along exactly what we're going to do about the sand dunes tomorrow?"

Clayburn nodded. "Passed along them when I was riding south. It's windy this time of year, and the wind keeps shifting the dunes, sweeping some parts almost clear. And we can bull through the parts that aren't clear, if we tackle it the right way."

"If we do," Cora said slowly, "that'll mean we'll be out of the desert ahead of Adler."

"Uh-huh." Clayburn's forehead creased. He finished the coffee in his cup and set it down carefully. "I expect that's when Adler will hit at us."

Cora frowned at him. "You sound very sure of it. But we've been on the trail for over a week now and nothing has happened."

"For reasons," Clayburn said. "First of all we were still too near Parrish most of the week. Adler would wait till we're well beyond reach of the law. He'd wait, too, in hopes we might break down without interference from him. And this country's too flat—you can see riders coming at you from a long way off. When we get into the hill and canyon country, and he finds out we've made it and he's behind us—that's when he'll do something about us."

"You sound as if you know exactly when he'll do it, and how. And exactly what we'll do to stop him."

Clayburn shook his head. "Not exactly. It'll depend on the time and place."

She stared at him in silence for a few seconds. "You know, Clay, you act like you can read every thought in Adler's head. And I've got a hunch you can."

Clayburn hunched his heavy shoulders and smiled meaninglessly. "If you play against a man, it only makes sense to put yourself in his place and figure out what you'd do if you were him. Everybody does that."

"No. Everybody *tries*. It's like that little poker session of ours. I was concentrating on tricking you—while you had already thought out what I was doing and what to do about it."

Haycox, sitting stiffly on the other side of Cora, spoke up suddenly. "Clayburn, I hope you turn out to be as good at fighting as you're supposed to be at thinking long thoughts."

Cora looked at Haycox. "You've *seen* him fight."

"With his fists," Haycox drawled. "But next time it'll have to be with guns. You've hired a fine bunch of brawlers, Cora. I'm just wondering how they'll stand up to bullets."

Jim Roud had drifted over while they were talking. He grinned down at Haycox. "Don't worry yourself about that, gunfighter. We can all handle ourselves if it comes to shooting, too."

Haycox gazed up at him sardonically. "Can you? From what I heard, being a deputy in Parrish didn't give a man much practice with a gun. There was always Marshal Kavanaugh to hide behind."

Roud's ugly face flushed.

Clayburn said, quickly and softly, "Easy, Jim . . ."

Roud glanced down at him, controlled himself, and shifted his glance to Haycox. "Want a demonstration?" He pointed with his left hand to a small rock just near enough to be seen in the failing evening light. "Watch it."

His right hand blurred, whipping the Colt up out of his holster. It fired as it cleared leather. The rock jumped, breaking down the middle into two fragments.

He looked again at Haycox. "Good enough?"

Haycox shrugged a thin shoulder. "Not *too* bad. Sure it's the best you can do?" He stood up with a swift, uncoiling motion, his hands poised over the butts of the two guns strapped low to his thighs. "You looked a little slow to me. Try again."

Roud hesitated, then slipped the Colt back in his holster. "Okay." He spread his feet, eyes focusing on one of the two pieces of rock, his compact figure hunching for a fast draw. Then he made his move, faster than the last time.

Both of Haycox's hands moved at the same time. His guns seemed to spring into them. They roared simultaneously, before Roud's gun was even clear of its holster.

The two rock fragments smashed into bits.

Without bothering to look at Roud, Haycox turned to Clayburn. "Maybe *you'd* care to try it?"

"What for?" Clayburn asked in a bored voice.

"I'd like to know just how good you are."

Clayburn showed his teeth in a kind of a smile. "Then we'd *both* know, wouldn't we?" He shook his head. "Nope. It's a waste of scarce ammunition."

The gunman's thin face tightened. "If you're expecting trouble from Adler, some target practice for everybody wouldn't be a bad idea."

Clayburn stood up, dusting his hands on his thighs. "Anybody that needs target practice at this point, doesn't have enough time left to learn."

He motioned to Roud and sauntered off to check the corralling of the horses and mules.

Cora Sorel rose to her feet beside Haycox. "You two certainly don't seem to get along very well."

He turned on her angrily. "And you and him seem to get along too damn well."

Amusement quirked her lips. "Jealous?"

His empty eyes fastened on her face. "You know how

you acted with me in Parrish,'' he said tightly. ''Not like that time in Butte when you wouldn't let me get near you. That's why I came along on this stupid job. And you know it.''

Cora patted his cheek softly. ''I know.''

''If I thought you were just stringing me along for the use of my guns . . . making me wait for something that's not going to be . . .''

She smiled at him. ''Simmer down, honey. You'll find out if I meant it or not, when we get to Bannock.''

The promise he thought he saw in her eyes mollified Haycox. But not entirely.

An hour after dawn the next day the wagon train came to the sand-dune barrier stretching from horizon to horizon across their path. Clayburn was there waiting for them, having set out before dawn to hunt the best way across. He stood by his big sorrel horse between two dunes that rose like brownish waves more than six feet above his head, their crests rippling in the steadily moaning wind.

The brim of his hat was tugged well down over eyes narrowed to slits, and he'd tied a bandana across the lower part of his face to keep the flying sand out of his nostrils and mouth. As the others neared the undulating dunes and felt the stinging lash of the wind-whipped grains of sand, they followed his example.

He gathered the men and stated the situation flatly. ''There's no easy way across. So we'll try it where it's narrowest, which is right here. It's about a two-mile haul. Some spots have been blown almost clear. But there're longish stretches where it's pretty deep that'll take some doing. Let's get started by double-teaming the first four wagons.''

Because the chuck wagon was much lighter than the freight wagons, he'd decided on testing the route across by taking it through first. While the teamsters unhitched the mule teams from the last four freight wagons and joined them to the teams of the first four, the chuck wagon got rolling. Roud had taken over the driver's seat. Clayburn and the powerful Kosta went on foot, leading the first of the team horses and pulling them along when they hit the sand drifts between the dunes.

In a couple of places they got bogged down, but were able to wrench the chuck wagon free. In one place the sand finally proved too soft and deep to get through, and they were forced to search out a detour where it was more solidly packed down underfoot. But they managed to get to the other side of the dunes in a little under an hour.

It was going to be much slower going, Clayburn knew, with the capacity-loaded freight wagons. Leaving Roud to guard the chuck wagon and give warning with his gun of any trouble approaching from that side, Clayburn and Kosta trudged back across the dunes.

They found the first four wagons ready to be hauled through by their doubled teams of mules. The difficulty of the way across decided Clayburn on taking the wagons one at a time. Assigning Haycox to stand guard on this side, he and Kosta guided the lead mules of the first wagon into the dunes. The teamsters from the other wagons followed on foot.

Halfway through, the mules and wagon wheels sank so deep in loose sand that they were brought to a dead halt. The teamsters grouped around the wagon, put their backs and shoulders to it and began pushing. With them straining every ounce of strength, with Kosta and Clayburn pulling for all they were worth, and with the mule-skinner spurring the teams to renewed efforts by the stinging snap of his long whip, the freight wagon budged forward again, balking against every gained inch.

At one point Clayburn saw Cora had joined the grunting, heaving teamsters in pushing the wagon. He knew the little she added wouldn't accomplish much, but she was probably doing the right thing. It kept her too occupied to worry; and the sight of a woman pitting herself against the sand and the heavily resistant wagon drove the teamsters into using more muscle than they'd thought they had in them.

They kept the wagon moving. But every foot of the way

cost a mountain of toil. When they finally got to the other side where Roud waited, the mules were trembling with exhaustion in their traces.

Clayburn immediately led the men back through the dunes, not allowing them time to find out just how tired they were.

They bulled the second double-teamed wagon through the way they had the first—and went back for the third. It was time for the midday meal when they got the fourth wagon across.

The food and rest gave the men a chance to realize how worn-out they were—and to get over it somewhat. Clayburn was relieved to find that he didn't have to force any of them to their feet when he called an end to the meal break.

By then the mules that had hauled the first wagon through had recovered. They were unhitched and led back through the dunes to be hitched to the fifth wagon. This time it was even slower work getting the wagon across. But they got it done. Then the mule teams that had pulled the second wagon were used to haul the sixth one.

Clayburn was surprised—and impressed—to find Cora Sorel still with them, shoving against the wagon with the weariness-weakened teamsters. And when they went for the seventh wagon she still didn't drop out. She looked pale and shaken, and half out on her feet. But Clayburn didn't try to persuade her to call it quits. It was her cargo they were taking to Bannock. It was her money that would be lost if they didn't get there.

Dusk was closing around them when they got the last wagon across the dunes. It had taken an entire day to traverse just two miles.

Clayburn was gambling that the total time saved by taking the shorter route through the desert would make up for it.

They were entering a land of rugged hills, mesas and rock canyons two days later, the wind growing steadily colder, when Ranse Blue caught up to them with news that Clayburn had won his gamble.

Adler's outfit was more than half a day behind them.

NINE

The sun was a dull red blob sinking into the jagged horizon, casting long tortured shadows across a landscape that might have been created by the dropping from the sky of a God-sized jigsaw puzzle of stone and clay; a land of flat-topped mesas and twisting canyons and towering masses of rock, of eroded butte spires, dry gullies and monstrous boulders. The wind was not strong, but its breath had become noticeably colder during the day's progress northward.

Clayburn sat his tall sorrel atop a high flat rock, the collar of his sheepskin coat turned up to warm his ears as he gazed north to the dark, looming range of the mountains. Snow gleamed on those mountains, tinged with a rosy hue by the setting sun. But it only showed in patches, high up, and the clouds above the range were light and fluffy, containing no threat of more snow. Not yet.

His saddle creaked under him as Clayburn turned slowly, taking one last survey of the other horizons. When he was studying the south, he became very still. Then he raised his field glasses to his eyes, adjusted them to the distance. There was dust rising behind the farthest rimrock.

It might be Apaches. But he'd spent most of that day hunting for sign of their presence, without finding any. Besides, it wasn't Apaches that he was expecting at this stage in the game.

The dust was blown away on the wind. No more rose

in its place. No riders appeared over the rimrock. Clayburn waited, watching through the high-powered lenses. Five minutes passed. Nothing further stirred back there. Finally Clayburn lowered the glasses, twitched the reins, and rode the sorrel down off the rock into a deep meandering gully.

Two hundred yards away, the red-haired Wilks crouched in the dark shadow of a boulder and watched him go. . . .

The dry gully led Clayburn into a crisscrossing of shallow canyons. He pulled up the sorrel and listened. Then he kicked his mount into motion again, cutting southwest through the canyon maze. Half a mile farther on he found the wagon train filing past the bottom of a vast shale slide, Cora and Roud riding flank and Haycox trailing a quarter of a mile behind the last freight wagon.

Cora rode up as he approached. She looked tired from the long day's riding, but she straightened on her buckskin and grinned as they met.

"You're a little late tonight, Clay. I was beginning to worry."

"About me?"

"You sound surprised. Are you supposed to be indestructible? Things *could* happen to you."

Clayburn nodded. "And have—too many times."

"Did you find a good place for us to camp for the night?"

"One that'll serve," he told her, and rode in ahead of the chuck wagon. Motioning Kosta to follow, he angled northeast away from the shale slide.

Keeping pace with him, Cora said, "I've been studying the ridges all around for two days straight, ever since you told me Adler had somebody watching us. I haven't seen a sign of anybody."

"Don't get your hopes up. He's there."

Involuntarily, Cora glanced off to left and right. Then she looked again at Clayburn's hard, impassive profile. "Where?"

He shrugged. "I don't know—because I've made a point of not looking."

The wagons were halfway through a deep, wide canyon when Roud caught up to Clayburn and Cora.

"I like the looks of this place, Clay. Two ways in or out, both real narrow so they'll be easy to defend. Walls too steep for anybody to come all the way down at us. Nice safe spot to camp in for the night."

"It is," Clayburn agreed. "But it's not where we're camping."

Dusk was growing into night when they emerged from the other end of the canyon, cut to the right, and came to a dead end. The area was hemmed in on three sides by low cliffs, from the base of one of which a spring trickled into a shallow water hole.

Clayburn raised an arm to halt the wagons. "This is it."

Roud stared around them dubiously. "Here? You usually know what you're doing, Clay, but take another look at that cliff rim up there. Be awful easy for anybody coming through the canyon to get up there and pick us off. And just as easy for the rest of Adler's men to come in at us. We'll be boxed in, no way out. It's a death trap."

Clayburn smiled wolfishly. "Looks that way, doesn't it?"

Wilks slipped back down the canyon to the horse he'd left hidden behind a group of boulders. He led the horse till he reached the other end of the canyon, well beyond hearing distance of Cora Sorel's outfit. Mounting up, he rode south through the deepening night. He did not push his horse too fast, but let it feel its way over the rock-strewn ground so that it wouldn't trip and break a leg. There was plenty of time. There was the whole long night ahead in which to finish the job.

A little over an hour later he found the place where Adler was waiting with the rest of his men and their horses.

Wilks swung down from his horse to face Adler. "Either you're a mind reader," he told his boss, "or you're mighty damn lucky."

"Talk straight," Adler snapped.

"You couldn't've picked a better night for it. They're camped inside a little box canyon. We won't even have to rush 'em. Just bottle 'em up in there, get our best shots on one of the rims above, and wait for dawn. Come first light, the boys on the rim can start picking them off like shooting ducks in a barrel. The walls're low enough for that, but too steep for anybody to get up at us. They'll only have one way out and the rest of us'll be waiting there for them, nice and safe behind some rocks, to cut 'em down as they come out."

"Sounds easy," Adler said, half to himself.

"A picnic."

"A little too easy."

Wilks laughed softly, his teeth showing in the starlight. "You'd like it better if it was harder?"

Adler nodded slowly. "Maybe. Clayburn's no fool. He got Cora Sorel's wagons across the desert ahead of us. He outwitted you at that stage station. . . ."

"The hell he did," Wilks growled. "I did what I went there to do, didn't I? And got away clean—with all Clayburn's money in the bargain. You should have seen his face when I . . ."

But Adler was busy with his own thoughts. "If he knows you've been watching them all this time . . ."

"Not a chance. He didn't spot me once, didn't know I was around."

"You're very sure of that?"

"You just heard me say so. It's not the first time I've had to trail somebody without being seen, you know."

Adler nodded slowly, "All right. If you're sure. Take the men in. Get it done—and done right."

Wilks regarded him quizzically. "How about you?"

"I'll be here. Waiting."

It surprised Wilks. "How come? Never knew you to be scared to go into a fight before."

"And I'm not now. But this time my only concern is with getting my wagons to Bannock; and making sure mine are the only ones that get there before the snows. If I got myself shot down there'd be no point to any of this. *You're* the one's so sure this is going to be easy. And you're the one getting the bonus for stopping Cora Sorel's wagons."

"And taking all the chances," Wilks added cheerfully. "Okay. Just be ready to pay me that bonus tomorrow."

He turned from Adler to Benjy, Dillon and the others. "From the marks I saw on some of you I'd say Clayburn and his bunch had a lot of fun with you back in Parrish. Tonight it'll be your turn to have all the fun. . . . Let's go."

Ranse Blue found Cora Sorel's wagon camp by the light of its cook fires. He rode in on a tired horse, leading another that looked equally weary, cursing at a guard who demanded that he identify himself as he emerged from the darkness. Clayburn strode to meet him, followed by Cora, Roud and Haycox.

The old buffalo hunter, climbed down stiffly, looked around him at the low cliffs, and scratched his dirty gray whiskers. "Clayburn, you sure picked a helluva spot to receive visitors."

"They're coming?"

Blue turned his face slightly and spat at the ground. "They're comin', all right. Every damn one of 'em, except three Adler left behind with the wagons and mules. A helluva lot more men than we've got. And right now they're all sittin' just about an hour's ride from here. Waitin', I guess, for a fellow I spotted sneaking back down that canyon outside when I was comin' in."

"Did he spot *you*?" Clayburn asked quietly.

Blue gave him an offended look for an answer.

"Clay," Cora said anxiously, "Roud was right about this being a bad place to camp."

"He didn't say it was a bad place to camp," Clayburn told her. "He said it was a bad place to take an attack. But this isn't where we're going to take it. They've got to come through that long canyon out there to get here."

Roud grinned at him. "You sonuvabitch! I wondered what you were up to."

"Now you know. Get the men started pulling off that brush."

Roud hurried off to attend to the roped bundles of dry brush and dead twigs that Clayburn had set them to gathering and tying onto the wagons two nights back.

Clayburn turned back to Ranse Blue. "Are Adler's wagons still half a day behind us?"

"Nope. Not no more. *Less*, now. Adler's mules are fresher than ours. They didn't wear themselves down fightin' through those sand dunes like ours did. They're catchin' up on us. The rate Adler's closin' the distance, he'll be ahead of us again before we reach Bannock."

Haycox gave Clayburn an amused look. "It seems you weren't as smart as you thought."

Clayburn showed no sign of hearing him. "Then the time's come," he told Blue, "to slow Adler up some more. Get four fresh horses. Two for you, two for me. Take them all the way through the canyon and get out of sight with them past the other end. And whatever happens stay there till I come for you. It may take a while."

Blue's wrinkled face glared at him. "You expectin' me to do more riding tonight?"

"Uh-huh."

"Goddamn it, Clayburn, I need some sleep. Ain't had time for more'n a couple hours at a snatch ever since . . ."

Humor touched the corners of Clayburn's mouth. "Old men don't need much sleep. That's why I hired you. You can grab a nap while you're waiting for me—though it may get a little noisy for you before long."

"You sure expect a man to sweat blood for his pay," Blue complained. But he trudged off to pick out the four horses.

Clayburn's eyes settled on Haycox. "Speaking of pay," he said thinly, "the time's come to start earning yours."

TEN

They entered the long canyon riding two abreast—Wilks and Dillon in the lead, followed by Slope and Benjy with the rest of the men trailing behind, their guns ready. They made a formidable little army, and Wilks had already worked out how he would place each man.

The looming stone walls on either side of him shut out the starlight, making it so dark that Wilks could not see more than a couple feet ahead—and all he could see there was more darkness. And the way in was narrow, made narrower still by the piles of rocks and boulders jumbled against the base of the cliffs. But there was more than enough room for two horses to ride through side by side, and Wilks knew the way. He'd been through it twice while it had still been light, and his sense of direction was a keen one.

The narrow stretch at this end of the canyon was long. Wilks and Dillon were still in it when the two men bringing up the rear came into it. Wilks' thoughts were already farther down the canyon: Halfway through they'd dismount, out of earshot of Cora Sorel's camp. They'd go the rest of the way silently on foot. If they ran into any guards before getting into position the main body of his men would make a rush for it, depending on their superior numbers to get them to the rocks that would be their barricade. Otherwise they would quietly take up their position, ready to shoot down every man and animal trying to break out of the trap. He'd already picked his best marksmen to work their way onto the low cliff overhanging the wagon camp. And once they'd closed the trap . . .

Fifty yards to Wilks' left, Clayburn rested on one knee behind a mass of rock, his carbine cradled in both hands, his finger across the trigger. He couldn't see the riders moving slowly past him, except as shadowy disturbances of the general darkness. But he could hear them plainly, the creak of their leather and clop of their horses hoofs. He held himself in, waiting.

His men were scattered to his right and left behind the rocks. Jim Roud was the nearest to him on one side; Haycox was on his other side, almost in touching distance. It had taken some arguing to keep Cora from being with them. She'd finally settled for joining the two men assigned to the other end of the canyon, to pick off any attackers that got through here. Clayburn did not intend for many to get through.

The stone under his bent knee began to hurt. He did not move. He continued to watch the vague movement through the darkness, listening, waiting tensely. . . .

Wilks felt his horse begin to act strangely under him, trying to slow its walking pace. He glanced quickly to his left. But he could see nothing there, not even the rocks at the base of the canyon entrance wall. He stared straight ahead, still saw nothing, and kneed his mount to keep it moving. In the next few seconds they should be out of this narrow stretch. . . .

Then he saw something dead ahead. Nothing he could identify or even be sure was really there. It was only that part of the darkness there looked somehow more solid. Instantly Wilks reined his horse to a stop.

Beside him, Dillon was not so quick. His horse took two more steps forward, head-on into something that crackled and gave resistance. The barrier of ropes and dry brush stretched across the end of the canyon entrance.

Dillon's horse whinnied in fright and reared back from the barrier. The two men Clayburn had waiting there scratched matches on rock. Each set fire to a cloth-wrapped stick soaked in kerosene, and threw it.

Wilks already had his gun in his hand, hammer back, when matches touched kerosene. He fired at the flare of the nearest torch as it was thrown. His shot winged the man who threw it—but both torches fell straight into the middle of the brush barrier.

The next second the brush was on fire, its flames licking skyward, outlining Wilks and his mounted raiders.

Clayburn laid his carbine barrel across the top of the rock in front of him and fired at the nearest man revealed to him by the flames. The carbine stock recoiled into his shoulder. The bullet took the raider high on the side of his chest and tore him from his saddle. On either side of Clayburn the guns of his men crashed out, the barrage thundering against the confines of the canyon walls and slashing the raiding force apart.

Men and horses went down screaming. The orderly two-file line disintegrated into a churning mass of riderless horses, men on foot and still-mounted riders—all tangling with each other in a desperate scramble to get away from the blaze that revealed them to the defenders' gunfire.

The raiders were moving fast now, becoming more difficult targets frequently hidden by milling horses. But some of the defenders were firing at anything that moved, not caring if it was only men they hit. One was Haycox, earning his pay now with a vengeance, firing coolly with either hand. In the brief glimpse that Clayburn caught of him, one of his guns nailed a crawling man flat to the ground and his other gun bowled over a riderless horse stampeding straight at the rocks.

It was a slaughter, not a fight. Some of the raiders tried to shoot back. But they couldn't see what they were shooting at, and the rocks behind which the defenders crouched protected them from blindly fired bullets. Most of the raiders didn't even try. They concentrated on getting out of the canyon mouth, back the way they'd come in.

It was over in minutes. By the time the fast-burning brush consumed itself the last of the raiders were gone—leaving behind only those who would never go anywhere again.

The abrupt cessation of gunfire was a shock. Clayburn drew a hand over his eyes, shook his head to clear it, and climbed over the rocks. By the lowering light of the last flickering flames he moved swiftly among the dead, twice pausing to turn over with the toe of his boot a man who lay face down.

If Adler had been among them, he would have known the trouble was done with. He didn't find Adler. But he did find Benjy and Slope.

He stood for a moment longer staring at the dead while his men crowded out from behind the rocks and converged on him. His mouth was a tight bitter line and his heart thudded heavily in his chest. But when he raised his head his face was wooden, his eyes cold.

"What's our own damage?" he demanded in a tired voice.

"One man winged in the left arm," Kosta told him. "Fischman."

"That's all?"

Kosta grinned at him in the fading light. "That's all."

Clayburn nodded aimlessly, moved his shoulders, and began ejecting the used carbine shells.

Haycox asked, "Do you think they'll be back for more?" There was a little more respect in his voice now.

"No," Clayburn said tonelessly. "Not tonight. Not here. They know our position's too strong for the number of them left. We got too many of them; the odds are about even now."

He began reloading the carbine as he turned to Roud. "You're in charge till I get back, Jim. Keep a heavy guard here, so they can't trickle in and pull our own trap on us when you take the wagons out at dawn. And before you pull out have a look around, make sure they're not laying for you anywhere outside."

He was fairly sure they wouldn't be. The surviving raiders would be heading back to their camp now, to lick their wounds. And they'd be going slow. They'd lost more horses than men. Some of the raiders would have to ride double.

"When'll you be back?" Roud asked him.

"Sometime tomorrow. Don't wait for me anywhere along the route. Just keep pushing north. I'll catch up."

Clayburn snapped the last load into the carbine, levered a cartridge into firing position, and slipped away into the darkness to find Ranse Blue.

ELEVEN

With each man riding first one of his horses and then the other, Clayburn and Blue were able to keep going steadily at a fast, mile-consuming pace. It still lacked some three hours to dawn when they neared Adler's wagon camp.

They tethered the four horses half a mile away. Because it was certain that Adler's raiders couldn't have made it back yet, they left their rifles in their saddle scabbards. They moved on through the starlit darkness on foot, Blue leading the way deeper into a labyrinth of canyons and buttes.

Clayburn followed Blue down a gentle slope, treading with care so as not to displace any pieces of the loose shale. They moved past a group of massive clay formations shaped like giant mushrooms, entered a twisting stone corridor with curved sides almost coming together over their heads. As they reached the end of it Blue stopped, half-turning to touch a hand to Clayburn's ear. Clayburn nodded that he understood: they were now within hearing distance of the wagon camp.

From there on they moved with special care, both men walking Indian fashion, testing each step before putting full weight on it so as not to disturb any loose stones or snap a twig underfoot. They threaded their way in a crouch, keeping within the darkest shadows, crossing what had once been a deep river but was now a cracked and pitted expanse of hard-baked clay. Their boots making no sound at all, they went under a stone arch and through a narrow dry gulch bottomed with rocks.

Reaching the base of a low slope, Blue again paused, and made a downward motion with his hand against Clayburn's chest. Then Blue started up the slope on his hands and knees. Clayburn crawled after him. When Blue halted just below the top, Clayburn moved up beside him, and raised his head only enough to see over the rim.

Beyond the slope the ground leveled till it reached the looming side of a great mesa. Between the mesa and the slope was a scattering of boulders—and Adler's wagon camp.

Clayburn gave his full attention to the dark shapes of the big wagons. They were formed into a rough square, with all the mules corralled inside the square. There were too many mules for the square to contain them if the wagons touched end to end. So large spaces showed between each wagon—spaces across which ropes would be strung from one wagon to the next so the mules couldn't get out.

There was no campfire, nothing to see by but the starlight. And there was no sign of the three guards Adler had left behind. Clayburn stayed where he was, his eyes scanning the night-shrouded wagons in search of them. He was fairly certain that Adler was too smart to let his guards stay near the wagons, with all those boulders around the outside of the camp. But it would have been foolish to ignore the possibility.

He felt time pressing hard on him, urging him to hurry. They had to get done with it and be gone before Adler and his raiders returned to cut off their retreat. But to hurry at the expense of caution would be equally suicidal. Clayburn held himself in, forcing himself to take the time necessary. He had to know where at least one of the guards was before moving closer.

Finally, he transferred his attention from the wagons to the boulders closest to the camp area. Nothing moved anywhere. Clayburn remained where he was, waiting, watching. The coldness of the air and ground began making itself felt through his pants and coat. Time passed. His nerves were stretching taut. Still he lay motionless against the top of the slope, studying the boulders with pinpointed concentration.

Then he saw something move in the deep shadow of a boulder off to the right of the wagon camp. Not a man; not anything that could be identified. Just a movement.

Blue saw it at the same time. He touched Clayburn's elbow. Clayburn focused all his attention on the boulder. No one showed himself. The movement was not repeated.

But he knew he'd seen it. And that it meant one of the guards was there. That was all he knew. There was no way of guessing if the man was sitting or standing, or the direction in which he was looking.

Clayburn sucked in a slow, deep breath and went up over the rim of the slope on his belly. Any one of the three guards might be at that moment looking toward the slope. There was no help for that. All Clayburn could do was make himself as much a part of the ground as possible, and make no sound to attract attention his way. Raising all his weight on just his elbows and toes, his head down and the rest of him barely off the ground, Clayburn snaked toward the nearest boulder.

He reached it without anything happening, and once in its protective shadow let his breath out slowly and lowered himself full-out on the ground for a second's rest. Blue came up beside him in the same fashion, his presence neither heard nor seen, merely felt.

There were other boulders now between him and the one under which he'd seen the movement. But any one of them might hide one of the other guards. Clayburn studied the next nearest boulder intently, raised himself an inch on his elbows and toes, and worked his way toward it. It was a strenuous, tiring way to travel over even a short space. By the time he reached the next boulder he was clenching his bared teeth to still the sounds of his hard breathing.

Resting, he spared moments for another look around. It didn't buy him the location of either of the other guards.

There was now only one more boulder between him and

his objective. He stared at the deep shadow under it for long precious seconds, goaded by the awareness that Adler and his raiders were getting closer with each one of those seconds. When he was as certain as he could be that no one was on his side of the boulder, Clayburn snaked across the intervening space toward it.

Again he made it without anything happening. This time he did not pause when he reached the boulder, but continued around it in the shadow of its base, making sure there wasn't a guard against the other side of it.

Now there was nothing between him and the boulder where he'd seen movement. Nothing to hide him the rest of the way but the night. The pale shine of the stars seemed suddenly very bright.

In the shadow of the boulder where he'd seen movement before he could see none now. The man who had to be there was invisible. He might be standing or sitting; might be looking straight at Clayburn. . . .

Clayburn slipped his fingers inside his left sleeve and drew the knife from its sheath. Holding it point-forward, he began inching toward the boulder on knees and toes, his taut-held body almost brushing the earth as he moved.

This time he did not move in a straight line, but angled off to his left so that the bulk of the boulder would no longer be directly behind the guard in its shadow. Halfway across the open space Clayburn finally saw the vague shape of a man, detached slightly from the boulder itself, outlined against the star-filled sky.

The man was standing, leaning a shoulder against the side of the boulder, a rifle in the crook of his arm. He was tall, and seemed heavily built, but Clayburn couldn't be sure of his shape below the shoulders where it merged with the boulder. As Clayburn watched, the man's head turned. Clayburn froze against the ground. The man looked his way, but not down at the ground that close.

The instant the man's head turned away Clayburn moved again, slowly closing the distance between them. The man unfolded his arms, dropped the rifle to his hand. Clayburn froze again, then resumed his movement when the man only stretched, flexed his big shoulders, and transferred his rifle to the crook of his other arm.

The guard scratched the side of his face, glanced off toward the slope up which Clayburn and Blue had come, then looked past the wagons at the looming mesa.

By then Clayburn was almost under the man's feet. He came up off the ground like a tightly wound steel spring suddenly uncoiling. His left hand fastened on the guard's mouth to stifle any outcry and his right drove the point of his knife between the man's ribs next to the spine.

The guard's whole body convulsed. His rifle fell. Clayburn broke its fall with his boot to lessen the sound of it. He held the struggling man in an iron grip and forced the blade deeper in his back, twisting. The guard's struggles became weaker, uncoordinated, then ceased entirely.

Clayburn held the sagging weight and lowered it silently to the ground. For a second he remained bent over the dead body, his breath coming fast through his clenched teeth, his legs rubbery, his throat dry and a bitter taste in his mouth. Then he pulled the knife free and wiped it on the dead man's sleeve. He straightened against the boulder and looked around. There was nothing to indicate that the other two guards had been alerted, wherever they were.

Blue appeared beside Clayburn like a shadow. There was no need for whispers or motions between them now. Each new what to do next. Blue picked up the dead guard's rifle and held it ready. Clayburn left him, and the protection of the boulder, lowering himself to the ground and snaking toward the wagons.

He was almost there when the report of a rifle somewhere off to his left broke the night silence. A lead slug gouged a spout of dirt from the ground six inches from Clayburn's face. He sprang to his feet and sprinted the rest of the way in a low crouch, zigzagging as he ran. As he hit the ropes stretched between two of the wagons, the rifle boomed at him again.

The bullet chopped into the wagon tailboard next to Clayburn's shoulder. In the same instant Blue fired, aiming at the guard's rifle flash.

Clayburn saw the shadowy figure of a man detach itself from a boulder. The man stumbled forward two steps, fighting to stay on his feet and bring his rifle around for a shot at Blue. Blue fired again. The man pitched sideways and became a motionless shadow on the ground.

Another rifle crashed out from the rock rubble piled high against the base of the mesa. The slug spattered against the boulder behind which Blue had positioned himself. Clayburn turned swiftly to his job, slashing his knife through one of the ropes stretched taut between the two wagons, then cutting the other rope.

He went in through the opening, entering the corral formed by all the wagons. The mules were already stirring nervously, frightened by the gunfire. Clayburn smacked and elbowed the nearest ones to start them out through the opening he'd made. Then he slipped on to the next opening, slashed the ropes, and got the mules started through there.

Repeating this at a third space between wagons, Clayburn moved on and climbed up on a wagon wheel so he wouldn't get trampled. He drew his Colt and began firing it into the ground, showering dirt against the legs of the milling animals and terrifying them to more speed in their efforts to escape from the corral.

Two more rifle shots cracked from the rock rubble at the base of the mesa. This time they were fired at Clayburn. Which was foolish. The guard there couldn't see Clayburn; he was just firing at the sound of Clayburn's Colt. All he accomplished was to kill one mule and start another stamping and screaming with pain—which hurried still more the terrified exodus of the rest.

As the last of the mules stampeded out of the openings Clayburn had created, Blue began firing at groups of them that showed an inclination to slow down. The mules scattered as they ran, and the boulders scattered them still more. Some headed for the mesa, but not many. More ran into the canyons to the left and right. The largest number of mules headed straight for the slope, down it, and vanished from sight.

Clayburn left the wagon corral and sprinted after them, joined as he reached the boulders by Blue. The guard at the base of the mesa fired after them. But distance and darkness were against him. None of his shots came near either Blue or Clayburn.

They sighted the mules ahead of them as they went down the slope. Some were still running away, others were milling around. Several gunshots encouraged the milling ones to follow those that were racing away. They scattered in a number of directions, one group following the dry river bed, other groups dispersing into the area's maze of cross-cut canyons and gullies.

The first streaks of predawn grayness fingered the sky when Clayburn and Blue rode away. They'd done what they'd come to do. It would take Adler's men most of the day to track down all the mules and gather them in. And they'd be tired mules. By the time Adler got his wagon rolling again, Clayburn estimated, Cora Sorel's outfit would be at least a full day ahead of him.

There was no longer any chance of Adler's outfit catching up and passing them.

Unless something happened to hold up Cora's wagons.

TWELVE

By the time they caught up to Cora's wagon train shortly after noon, Blue was beginning to look sick with fatigue and the need to sleep. Clayburn had a used-up feeling inside him, himself; and he ached from the steady riding. Their horses, in spite of being exchanged often, were almost finished when they finally sighted the wagons ahead.

Cora Sorel had been riding the drag position, looking back anxiously more and more often as the day wore on. When she spotted them coming, she immediately wheeled her buckskin and raced back to meet them.

She was no longer the woman she'd been back in Parrish, Clayburn reflected as she pulled up beside them. Her riding clothes were sadly trail-worn and her glamour was covered by layers of dust. Wind and sun had got to her face and hands, making them darker and roughening her skin. But she was still quite a hunk of woman.

In a flat, tired voice Clayburn told her what they'd done with Adler's mules. Cora started to laugh, then checked herself and glanced back the way they'd come.

"They'll come after us again for sure now," she said slowly. "They'll want revenge."

"They'll want revenge," Clayburn agreed. "If they'll come after it I don't know. We've got about the same number of men now. They'd be bound to lose more in a fight, and they can't afford that any more than we can. Adler needs most of the men he's got left just to handle his wagons."

''Couple more days north,'' Blue put in wearily, ''and we can stop worrying about Adler givin' us trouble. He'll have to keep his men wherever his wagons are, to protect 'em. We're gettin' into Apache territory.''

''Damn!'' Cora said softy. ''Now we have to worry about Indians, too?''

''I warned you,'' Clayburn reminded her, ''back in Parrish.''

Cora sighed. ''Yes. You warned me.''

''You could have stayed behind.''

Cora's soft mouth became stubborn, her dark eyes fierce. ''I'm not afraid of your damn Indians. It's just that I don't like it. I don't have to *enjoy* the idea of an Apache attack, do I?''

Lines appeared at the sides of Clayburn's mouth and eyes. ''Nope. Don't enjoy it much myself.''

''What *I'd* enjoy,'' Blue announced irritably, ''is for right now to climb into one of them wagons and get some sleep.'' He glared at Clayburn. ''And that's what I'm gonna do.''

Clayburn nodded. ''Go ahead. I'll be joining you.''

''And just how long you gonna let me sleep before I gotta ride back to watch Adler's outfit some more?''

''You're not going back for a while,'' Clayburn told him, and looked away to the mountains looming ahead. ''From now on we'll need you closer to the wagons. Like you said, we're getting into Apache territory.''

The wagons were moving through a long, mile-wide canyon a couple hours before sunset when a large bunch of riders came into the end of the canyon behind them. Clayburn, feeling himself again with five hours' sleep under his belt, was riding drag when he looked back and spotted their dust. He swung his horse around and swiftly brought up his field glasses.

As he focused the lenses, the oncoming riders slowed, bringing their mounts to a walk. Ten of them rode in a straight line abreast, their rifles in their hands. Adler rode well ahead of them, with just a single man on either side of him. One of them was Dillon.

Clayburn held his glasses on the other man with Adler for a moment, till he made out the red hair and was sure: It was Wilks. And he was carrying in his left hand a long stick with a white cloth fluttering from it.

"Well, what d'you know," Clayburn murmured to himself. He lowered the field glasses and saw that Roud, Haycox and Cora had joined him.

"Adler?" Cora asked tightly.

"Uh-huh. They're carrying a truce flag."

"Truce?" Roud stared down the canyon. "I don't believe it."

"Neither do I," Haycox chimed in. "It's obviously a trick."

"Maybe." Clayburn wheeled his sorrel. "Let's form up and find out."

Within minutes he had the wagons drawn up for defense, with Cora and most of the men barricaded behind the wagons or big rocks, rifles ready.

Adler's ten-man line of riflemen had pulled to a halt. Adler continued to come on a way, with Wilks and Dillon. He stopped just within range of his riflemen. And Clayburn's.

Clayburn rode out to meet him, flanked by Roud and Haycox. He was sure that whatever Adler's eventual plans, he wouldn't start anything here and now. Their meeting place was halfway between the rifles of the two enemy groups. Whoever started anything, all the men in the middle could count on being hit.

Wilks grinned at Clayburn as the two three-man groups met. "Nice seeing you again, gambler. How're the cards treating you?"

Clayburn looked at him wooden-faced. "I'm not playing much—till I get my money back from you."

"Figure to?" Wilks asked insolently.

"Sure."

"Now?"

Clayburn shook his head slightly. "No."

"Why not?"

"You're carrying a truce flag. And it'll wait."

Wilks laughed. "It'll wait, all right. Till hell freezes."

"Not that long," Clayburn said, smiling thinly. "I'll have my money from you—if you're still alive when I come for you."

Wilks stiffened in the saddle, losing his grin. "Any time, gambler. Any time."

"Shut up," Adler growled at him. "We're not here to talk up more trouble between us."

"What are you here for?" Clayburn asked quietly.

"I need more men," Adler told him. "I've come to hire some."

Clayburn smiled with his mouth.

"It strikes you funny?" Adler said. "It shouldn't. I need more men and I'm willing to pay well to get them."

Clayburn looked at Dillon's thin, surly face, then beyond to where Adler's ten riflemen sat their horses. His green eyes returned to Adler. "Seems to me you've already got enough to get your wagons to Bannock for you."

Adler made an impatient gesture. "You know exactly what I'm after. And I want you, especially. I'll pay you exactly three times whatever you're getting now, to switch sides."

Clayburn said, "No."

"You make up your mind without thinking."

"I don't have to think about it," Clayburn told him in a bored voice. "I chose sides back in Parrish. You made it a permanent choice when you had your men jump me in that alley."

"You'd hold a little thing like that against me when I'm . . ."

"I hold it against you," Clayburn said emphatically.

Adler's cold eyes stared at him, saw that nothing would change his mind. Adler looked at Roud and Haycox. "My offer also includes you two. Triple pay."

Roud shook his head. "Clayburn answered you for me."

Haycox said, "It's a real attractive offer. Unfortunately, Miss Sorel happens to be a friend of mine."

''Friendship doesn't cost anything,'' Adler countered. ''Sure she'll still be a friend after you've finished doing what she needs you to do?''

''Be a little more careful how you talk,'' Haycox warned icily. ''I don't like your tone of voice.''

''You've got your answer,'' Clayburn told Adler. ''You want us to turn on our own men, and we've turned you down.''

Adler didn't budge. ''If that's what's worrying you, any of the rest of your men who want to come over to me are more than welcome.''

''At triple wages?''

Adler's smile had nothing of humor behind it. ''*Double* wages. Teamsters are not quite as valuable to me as men like you three.''

Clayburn's smile was equally lacking in warmth. ''You *must* be worried, to be ready to put out all that money.''

''I'm gambling on more than making up for it in Bannock.''

''Sure you would. If your wagons were the only ones to get there.'' Clayburn's smile widened. ''But they won't be. You aren't even going to get there first. Because the answer to your offer is still no.''

Adler looked past Clayburn toward the wagons. ''Your teamsters haven't heard my offer yet. They may feel differently about it.''

Clayburn was afraid of that. Jim Roud just wasn't the kind of man who switched sides in the middle of a fight, and Haycox had his reasons for being loyal to Cora. But the rest of the men were another matter. They were good enough men, but money was money. Double pay was bound to weigh heavier than loyalty with some of them. And he couldn't spare any of them. Which was Adler's idea: without teamsters Cora couldn't move her wagons any farther.

''I'm answering for them,'' he told Adler flatly. ''No.''

Adler's lips thinned. ''I'll take the answer from *them*.''

Clayburn shook his head. ''You're not going near *them*.

And if you try shouting your offer, I'll put a bullet in your stomach before you get the second word out."

Dillon's hand moved closer to his holster. "That'd buy you a hole in your own gut."

"Maybe. But your boss would be beyond getting any pleasure out of that. Besides"—he inclined his head at Haycox—"I've got a fellow here that'd shoot your eyes out before you cleared leather."

Wilks said quietly, "I don't think so."

Haycox looked at Wilks. "You can find out, easy enough."

"Maybe you didn't notice," Dillon put in nastily, "those men we got behind us. And you're in real easy rifle distance if . . ."

"Shut up," Adler told him tonelessly. "We're *all* too exposed out here."

"That's a fact," Clayburn agreed amiably. "And none of us feel like bucking those odds against living. Do we?"

"You're the one," Adler pointed out, "that said you'd start shooting if I tried to contact your men."

Clayburn nodded. "That's what I said."

"Go ahead," Wilks urged his boss. "He doesn't mean it. He wouldn't have the nerve to risk it."

But Adler was studying Clayburn's face and deciding that he did mean it.

"Good-by," Clayburn said politely. "Time for you to turn around and go back. Been nice discussing things with you."

Adler stared at him a moment longer, then turned his mount and started away slowly. Dillon and Wilks backed their horses off a few paces, then wheeled to join Adler.

When they were out of earshot Wilks looked at Adler. "Do we hit them?"

Adler was staring straight ahead of him, his face brooding. "No. We don't have enough men for an open attack."

"It'll be night soon. We can sneak in and . . ."

"They're too ready for it. As you learned the last time you tried it."

Wilks' jaw clenched irritably. "Then we've wasted a

hell of a lot of time riding up here and back. "We'll be *two* days behind 'em after this."

"Not for too long," Adler said heavily. "And this hasn't been a waste of time. I'm this much nearer to Bannock."

He looked at Wilks. "I'll keep riding south with you till it gets dark, in case one of them is trailing us. Then I'll leave you. You're in charge of keeping the wagons moving till I get back. I'll take Dillon's horse with me, too. He can ride double with you back to the wagons."

Wilks frowned. "Where're you going?"

"Bannock. Using both horses I can be there in three days. At the rate the wagons move, that'll still leave me plenty of time."

"For what?"

"They'll be watching for us to hit them from the south. If they send a scout back to look, he'll see all of you are sticking with my wagons. And they'll figure their worries are over. They won't be expecting me to hit them from the north. . . . *That's* why I'm going to Bannock. I'm going to buy me some more men. And bring them back down with me."

Wilks scratched the side of his jaw. "You'll have to buy an awful lot of them."

"No," Adler said softly. "Not too many. Not for what I've got in mind."

"Adler made an offer," Clayburn told Cora when they returned to the wagons. He was aware of the other men there watching, and listening. But he looked only at Cora. "He said he was still willing to buy your freight, with the wagons and mules. Parrish prices."

Cora showed her surprise. "*That's* what he wanted?"

"Uh-huh. I told him you wouldn't be interested. But if I was wrong you can still . . ."

"You weren't wrong. He must be crazy to think I'd throw away my cards now that I've got a winner's hand."

"Not crazy. Just anxious."

"What will he do now?"

"I'm not sure. If he wants to try another attack, tonight's his best time for it. He can't keep riding his men back and forth between his wagons and ours. Every time he does, his freight'll get left farther behind."

"Then if he doesn't come tonight we're free of him?"

Clayburn shook his head. "I didn't say that. There's a number of other things he could do, and no knowing which he will do. We'll have to be on our guard all the way—against Adler, against Apaches. And deal with trouble as it comes."

Clayburn chose their campsite for that night with special care. After the evening meal he had the cook fires doused and gave orders that no more were to be lit till dawn. He assigned a full half of his men to guard duty among the rocks surrounding the wagon camp; at midnight they'd be relieved by the other half of the men. It meant that everyone would have to do with only half a night's sleep. But for the next few nights they would have to pay that price for security.

With the coming of darkness Clayburn saddled his sorrel and rode away—to circle the area until Blue relieved him at midnight.

When he was gone, Cora carried her bedroll away from where the men were bedding down, as she'd done every night on Clayburn's orders. Out of sight of the men she found a hummock that suited her. She was spreading the ground blanket when the figure of a man materialized in front of her.

She straightened quickly, her hand whipping to the Colt on her hip. Then she saw it was Haycox.

"Oh," she murmured, relaxing, "it's you. You'd better go get your sleep. You'll be . . ."

"I don't need much sleep," Haycox said, speaking just quietly enough so his voice would not carry to the men. "Never did."

"Well, I do. So if you don't mind . . ."

"I thought you'd like to know what Adler was after."

"Clay said . . ."

"He lied." Haycox came closer to her. "Adler offered us three times what you're paying to go over to his side."

"Why didn't Clay say so?"

"I'd guess he didn't want your teamsters to hear about it. Adler was willing to pay twice as much as you to any of *them* that'd switch sides."

Cora was silent for a moment. "Clay was right not to say so. Double pay's a lot of money."

"Triple is even more."

She tried to make out his expression through the shadows. "Tempted?"

"Not by Adler," Haycox told her in a gently mocking voice. "You know what I'm tempted by." He reached out and touched her with his open hand. "You feel like you look—soft but . . ."

She jerked away from his hand. "Don't!" she whispered fiercely.

"Why not?" His voice was quiet and probing. "Nobody can see us here. Back in Parrish you let me believe you feel about me like I do about you."

"And I've told you since—wait till we get to Bannock."

Haycox shook his head once. "Bannock's too long to wait to find out."

His hands seized her shoulders, dragging her to him. She struggled silently, twisting her face away. His fingers sank deeper into her shoulders, hurting. She went stiff and still. His mouth bruised viciously against hers, forcing her lips open. One of his hands moved down the small of her back, fingers cupping greedily.

Something small and hard and round pressed against his flat stomach.

He let her go abruptly, stepped back. Cora's gun was in her hand.

"So that's how it is," Haycox said in a flat, empty voice.

"I won't be manhandled," Cora whispered shakily. "I had more than I can take of that once. And I'll never let it happen again. Nobody touches me unless I let him know I want to be touched."

"And you don't want. Not by me. That's what I had to find out. You've been stringing me along. Adler was right."

"Adler? What did he say . . ."

But Haycox turned away without another word and vanished in the dark.

It took Cora a long time to fall asleep that night. When she woke at dawn she half expected to find Haycox gone.

But he was still there. And when he looked at her his face was expressionless. She could read nothing of what he was thinking.

Ranse Blue rode in when the mules were being hitched to the wagons and told Clayburn he'd followed the trail of Adler and his men for a way.

"They're gone—back south to Adler's wagons. All except one that took off with a spare horse, circled past us to the east over there. I reckon Adler detailed him to keep an eye on us, like before."

Clayburn's nod had no special meaning to it. He didn't say anything.

Blue fingered his whiskers thoughtfully. "I'd say Adler was callin' it quits—if it wasn't for him sending a man to keep track of us again."

"Adler hasn't quit," Clayburn said. He looked at the snow in the mountains ahead, and the big dark clouds that had formed over them during the night. "It'll take us ten more days to get to Bannock. More if those snow clouds really let go. That's a lot of time for something to happen in."

THIRTEEN

The winter snow began to fall their second day into the mountains. There were only small flurries at first, coming before noon while the mules were struggling to haul the heavy freight wagons up between thickly forested slopes. The trail was made difficult by tangles of dead trees and branches that had tumbled down the slope, and the snow flurries didn't help.

It stopped snowing after about an hour. Cora's wagon train continued slowly upward, aiming at a pass that showed only as a distant notch between two jagged peaks rising above the timberline. Late that afternoon there was another snow flurry. This one lasted less than half an hour. But Clayburn, squinting upward, knew it was only a prelude. The clouds had merged during that day into one solid overhang that completely blotted out the sky.

That night it grew much colder, and snow fell steadily for a couple of hours. At dawn the wagons and the land around them carried a layer of white. The sky was still overcast and there was the taste and smell of more snow in the air. Which meant harder going.

Looking over the men, Clayburn saw that the past nights of getting only half their sleep had taken their toll of them. He announced that they were going back to alternating three-man watches that night. It was risky, but necessary. Sleepy, fagged-out men couldn't handle mule teams over rugged terrain, or be fully ready when trouble came.

Ranse Blue returned in time for breakfast from an absence of a day and a night, with news that Adler's wagon train was in the mountains too.

"They're following another trail," he told Clayburn while he ate. "Over that way." He nodded eastward. "Good as this one; and shorter."

Clayburn nodded, looking to the east, "I know. I scouted it. There're some long, narrow ledges they'll have to go over farther on that'll get blocked up if it snows steady for a couple days. Not worth the risk."

Blue swallowed a mouthful of coffee, blinked as the heat of it brought tears to his eyes. "They're comin' along at a good pace so far. But it'll be another day and a half before they get as far north as we are right now."

Clayburn turned to him. "See any Apache sign?"

"Uh-huh. But old sign. How about you?"

"Same thing. Indian pony tracks, made about a week ago."

Blue glanced reflectively at the surrounding peaks and ridges. "Means they ain't close. Also means they're around us somewhere."

"I'd give something to know exactly where. . . . By the way, what took you so long? You should have been back last night."

"I decided to do my sleepin' on the trail," Blue told him nastily. "You usually got more work for me soon's I show up."

"That's so," Clayburn admitted, and stood up dusting snow from his trousers. "Right now you can finish filling your belly and get to work riding flank over on the left."

He assigned Roud to the right flank, Haycox to ride drag, and rode on ahead as the wagons got moving.

The wagon train entered the pass after the midday meal. Clayburn was scouting well in advance when it began to snow again. At the same time he spotted the tracks of an unshod pony crossing his path.

They led to the east, and unlike others he'd spotted these were fresh tracks, their imprints sharp in the frosted snow and beginning to fill up with the new snow. Clayburn's head turned quickly, his narrow eyes following them to where they vanished behind the curtain of falling snowflakes. His strong cheekbones and the line of his jaw became more prominent. He drew the carbine from its scabbard, reined his sorrel to the right, and followed the tracks.

He rode tensed, knowing that his prey might also be hunting him. Visibility was cut by the big soft flakes coming down steadily in the windless air, increasing the danger of being ambushed. It forced him to move slowly, though the tracks were filling up fast.

He had followed them for half an hour, as they cut around to the south, when they finally disappeared, blanketed under the fresh snow. Clayburn pulled up and for a few moments scanned the white world around him. Then he rode on through the maze of snow-shrouded boulders and pines, circling behind the wagon train and up the other side of it. He came across no further sign of his Indian.

Coming in sight of the wagon train from the west, Clayburn caught up to Ranse Blue riding flank.

"I just hit the tracks of an Indian pony," he informed Blue flatly. "Nice fresh ones this time."

Whatever the effect of this on the old buffalo hunter, he didn't show. "You were wonderin' where they were. Now you know."

"No," Clayburn said slowly. "I only know *one* of them's too close for comfort."

Blue looked at him sourly. "Never knew an Apache to travel alone—not for long. You're a bettin' man. I'll give you odds there's more where he came from, not more'n five hours ride from here."

Clayburn shook his head. "I don't bet against a pat hand."

"He'll just have himself a good look at us, make sure how many guns we got before hightailin' it off to his war party with the good news. Then they'll all be payin' us a visit."

"Maybe. Depends how many guns *they've* got."

Clayburn was looking across the moving wagons to the east. Jim Roud was supposed to be over there, riding the other flank. He wasn't there. In spite of the falling snow he should have been close enough to be seen.

"Where's Roud?" Clayburn asked tightly.

Blue looked off in the same direction, and scowled. "Dunno . . . He was over there last time I looked."

"Exactly where'd you see him last?"

"Back there by that break in the rocks. Where the big lightnin'-blasted pine is." Blue did not point. "Maybe Roud saw somethin' in there and went for a closer look."

"Yeah . . . that's what I'm afraid of. I'll go look for him."

"Maybe I better come with you."

"No. Stick with the wagons. If I'm not back by dark, pick a safe campsite."

"And if you don't come back—ever?"

"I'll be back," Clayburn told him as he turned his sorrel away. "Only the good die young."

"You're gettin' older by the minute," Blue said, but Clayburn was already out of earshot.

He didn't ride directly to the east. Instead he went west until Blue was swallowed up behind him by the falling snow. Then he turned south, riding a long circle behind the wagons. He cut north again when he was well east of the wagon train, beyond sight of it.

When he came to the narrow defile through the rocks where Blue had last seen Roud, Clayburn stopped his horse and dismounted. He tethered the sorrel inside a thick stand of high juniper and continued on foot, taking his carbine with him. Moving in a crouch that gave him the protection of the rocks and bushes along the way, he came in sight of the split and charred pine trunk Blue had mentioned. He squatted behind a clump of gooseberry bushes and scanned the bottom of the defile that cut east from the pass.

If Jim Roud had turned away from the wagon trail there, his tracks had been smothered under the falling snow.

Clayburn remained where he was for a time, considering the possibilities; not liking any of them. Then he moved on, keeping just below a humped line of ridge, following the direction of the defile. His finger was taut against the carbine's trigger guard. Every twenty yards he paused to scrutinize all possible cover within sight. The defile widened and grew deeper, then opened into a cross-cut ravine through which a shallow rock-choked stream rushed down through the mountains. Clayburn eased himself into a cluster of snow-covered rocks for a look into the ravine below.

Jim Roud lay face down in the stream, the back of his head and body showing above the white foam of the water. His arms and legs were sprawled out from him, toes touching the near bank, hands almost reaching the other bank.

A heavy knot formed in the pit of Clayburn's stomach. His eyes dulled. The lines of his face became slack, then slowly hardened again.

He bellied down in the snow and stayed that way, very still. Roud was dead and nothing could be done for him. To go down to his body now would be pointless, and could be suicidal.

Roud's horse was not in the ravine. Clayburn studied the dense thicket of pine, juniper and balsam on the other side of the stream. The Apache might have taken Roud's horse and be on his way by now. But Clayburn didn't think so. Thinking with the mind of an Apache, if he had killed Roud he would wait within sight of the body—long enough to see if anybody came looking for Roud.

If a single man came searching, he would wait till the man got to Roud's body. Then there would be two bodies in the stream, and two horses to take away as booty—something for a warrior to boast of for the rest of his life.

If more than one man came, an Apache could easily slip away in that thick forest on the other side.

Clayburn stayed where he was, hidden among the rocks, not moving though the intense cold began to numb the flesh of his face and hands. He scanned the thicket opposite for any unnatural line of shadow, any snow dropping from a shaken bough. He saw nothing, but he was a very patient man on occasion. Snow began to cover him, merging his form with the general whiteness all around.

The limit of the time the Apache would wait was reached, and passed. The wagon train was getting farther away. If anyone was going to come looking for Roud, he should have come by now. It was time for the Apache to relinquish his ambush position and take word of the wagon train to his bunch.

Clayburn continued to wait, gambling that someone *was* there on the other side of the stream, and that he wouldn't go off by merely fading deeper into the forest. There were easier ways out of the ravine, for a mounted man.

He was giving himself ten more minutes of waiting when a dense tangle of balsam on the other side of the stream betrayed movement within. An Apache warrior emerged astride a spotted pony, leading Roud's horse and carrying a rifle in one hand. He paused for a glance at Roud's body in the stream, and a swift survey of the surrounding area. His searching glance moved directly over the rocks among which Clayburn lay, without seeing anything that alerted him.

Clayburn could have shot him then. He wanted to. But he wanted more to find out first the location and size of the band the Apache belonged to. He waited till the Apache turned his pony and started up the ravine along the stream bank. Then he squirmed backward out of the rocks and hurried to his horse. Mounting up, he rode into the defile. Reaching the ravine, he crossed the stream without looking at Roud's corpse.

When he got to the other side, he found that the snowfall was already obscuring the trail left by the Indian pony and Roud's horse. Clayburn kneed the sorrel to a faster pace, squinting ahead to make sure he didn't approach within sight of his quarry. When the tracks became more distinct he slowed the sorrel a bit, but not too much.

It was dangerous, trailing an Apache warrior that close. Apaches had a habit of watching their back trail, and they learned ambush technique from the cradle. But with it snowing like this, to drop back farther would be to risk losing the tracks entirely. Clayburn kept the distance between them what it was. But he rode with the carbine ready in his hand, his finger close to the trigger.

The Apache's trail led out of the north end of the ravine and cut east with the stream. It entered an expanding gorge with rising walls along which stunted scrub pine sank roots among great outcroppings of rock. Clayburn followed the tracks east for over an hour. Then they turned north, still following the stream.

The stream angled and twisted, now east, then north again. Following the tracks beside it, Clayburn caught sight of a pass farther east of him—the pass up which Adler's wagons would be coming. The stream—and the Apache's trail—cut nearer to the pass, then away from it, continuing upward through the mountains in the same general direction as the pass but never exactly parallel to it.

The approach of dusk began to make itself known—early because of the overcast sky. About the same time the falling snowflakes diminished. It continued to snow, but less thickly. This meant that the tracks Clayburn was following filled up more slowly. He was able to see them farther ahead—and at the same time drop farther behind the Apache without losing his trail.

But it also increased the danger of the Apache seeing that he was being followed.

Before long Clayburn began to suspect that the Apache *had* spotted him. The tracks ahead cut away from the stream for the first time, angling up a rugged incline toward a high, long cliff. As Clayburn left the stream behind and approached the cliff he saw the farthest tracks led into a break in a massive outcropping of rock.

He slowed his horse, studying the outcropping through the lightly falling snow. There didn't seem to be any way out of it. His hunch that the Apache was laying an ambush for him began to pluck more determinedly at his nerves.

Of course, he could be wrong. But he'd learned long ago that it was healthier to have all your wrong hunches on the safe side. Twisting the reins, Clayburn angled the sorrel away from the direction of the Apache's trail, aiming for a place a bit to the left of where it entered the rock outcropping.

He kept the sorrel to a walk until just within accurate rifle distance of the rocks, considering the difficulty of aiming through the falling snow. Then, abruptly, Clayburn wrenched the reins right, kicked hard with his heels, and kept kicking. The sorrel leaped to its right and broke into a flat, all-out gallop. A split second later a rifle shot cracked out—much too late. A spout of snow rose and collapsed yards behind the speeding horse.

Hunched low over the sorrel's neck, Clayburn kept it racing for all it was worth, wrenching it now to the left, now to the right, in an utterly unpredictable zigzag course. Twice more the Apache fired at him. One shot kicked up snow under the sorrel's belly. The other winged over his back. Seconds after the last shot Clayburn and horse were under a shielding overhang at the base of the outcropping. The only thing the Apache's shots had accomplished was to let Clayburn know where he was.

Without pausing, Clayburn slid from his horse and sprinted to the left till he reached a tight little gully leading upward. He climbed upward swiftly, hugging the bottom of the gully to conceal himself below its shallow sides. The problem was that just as he knew in general where the Apache was, so the Apache had a good idea of where Clayburn was. And the Apache was bound to be swiftly changing his position, too.

By the time the gully came to an end under a big spur of rock, Clayburn could only be sure that his enemy was still somewhere to his right. He scanned the convoluted and haphazard formations in that direction as much as possible without showing himself. The Apache was nowhere in sight, and there were dozens of folds and crannies where he might be.

According to the strategy of such a hide-and-seek duel, the Apache should at that moment be working his way up higher among the rocks. The man higher up always had the advantage, the better chance of spotting the man below first.

Clayburn hesitated. Then, instead of continuing upward himself, he crawled under the spur and began working his way to the right. He moved with infinite caution, seeking the protection of overhead ledges and projections, pausing every few seconds to look behind him and through cracks and openings above. Where necessary he squeezed himself under giant fists of rock or crawled through narrow fissures—always conscious that the Apache might suddenly appear where he wasn't looking, with a clear shot at him. He was aware of an intensifying sensation of numbness in the small of his back, as though the nerves there were preparing themselves for the expected sudden impact of a fast-moving chunk of lead.

But he also knew that his enemy would be under the very same strain. They were each both hunter and hunted.

When he was several yards past the area from which the Apache had fired at him, Clayburn stopped and studied the rocks above. If his calculations had been right, his man was somewhere up there, and looking in the other direction for him. If so, there was a chance of coming up behind him, or at least getting close to him without being spotted. Uncomfortable *ifs*, but ones by which he would have to live or die.

Clayburn began working his way upward, the carbine gripped tight in his right hand. He found a tight, jagged seam in the face of the rock leading upward, and used it. He climbed slowly, careful to make no sound. The way became steeper, and he had to seek holds for his feet, his free hand and his right elbow, slowing his progress still more. Hauling himself up that way, having to hang on to keep from falling, he was sharply conscious of how defenseless he'd be in the vital first split second if the Apache spotted him.

Relief flowed through him when he finally reached the upper end of the seam. He rested on a narrow little ledge under a massive shoulder of rock, breathing through bared teeth till the action of his lungs became less violent. Then he wiped sweat from his eyes and surveyed the jungle of rock formations around him.

The Apache should be somewhere to his left now, perhaps a bit higher or lower, but close. Clayburn got his feet under him and started working his way to the left, crouching so low that his chest almost touched his knees. He placed his feet with care so as not to set any of the snow shifting downward to betray his position. He came to a twisted stone pinnacle that barred his way, began moving around it under a high ledge.

A dusting of snow fell on his hat and shoulders.

Clayburn whipped part way around, his right foot scraping on bared rock under it, his carbine smacking to his shoulder as he brought it up to fire at the ledge above.

There was nothing up there but a slight stirring of wind.

Clayburn had barely started to turn back to his original position when the Apache materialized three feet in front of him. The Apache stepped out from the other side of the stone pinnacle, bringing his rifle around for a point-blank shot at Clayburn as he made the step.

There was no time for Clayburn to bring his own carbine to bear. In the same instant that the Apache appeared he instinctively did the only thing left to him. He wrenched himself forward and around to his left, swinging the carbine in a swift, vicious arc like a club, getting all the power of his shoulders behind it. The barrel of the carbine thudded against the side of the warrior's neck.

The boom of the Apache's rifle and the sound of his neck snapping as he was knocked sideways against the pinnacle came together. Hot lead seared skin from Clayburn's side three inches below his armpit. The Indian crumpled like a puppet with all its strings cut.

Clayburn stared down at the Apache's inert form with a blank look on his face, breathing harshly, dizziness swirling in his head.

It lasted only seconds, then it was over. His brain steadied, and legs that had begun to tremble ceased to do so. Clayburn relaxed his grip on the carbine and straightened, looking out and down at the land below.

Roud's death had been avenged. But too soon, before the Apache had led him to the rest of his bunch.

Still—there was a possibility. He gazed thoughtfully at the stream below. His Apache had followed the stream this far. And the band he belonged to was likely to be camped near water. It would be dark in a little over an hour. Unless he and Blue had been wrong about how close the Apache party was likely to be . . .

Clayburn made his way back down. He found Roud's horse and took him along, releasing the Indian pony to wander off. He wasn't worried about the other Apaches finding it or their dead companion. By then the tracks leading back toward Cora's wagons would have been long obliterated. Mounting his sorrel and tugging Roud's horse along by a lead rope, he continued to follow the upward course of the stream. He rode warily, knowing it was more than an even chance the rifle shot had been heard by other Apaches.

He was a half hour's riding north of the Apache he'd killed when he saw a tendril of smoke rising ahead. Instantly turning away from the stream, Clayburn rode into a stand of pine. Hidden within the timber, he pushed on in the same direction. It was murky under the heavy overhanging boughs, and Clayburn let his horse go slowly, feeling its way around tangles of underbrush.

When the trees began to thin out on a steeply rising incline, the smoke was on Clayburn's left, between him and the stream. He kneed his horse up the slope. Higher up the timber became sparse and stunted, the incline became irregular with big sharp upthrustings of rock. Clayburn reached the top of the slope between two of the rock thrusts—and found himself looking down at the Apache camp.

It was near the stream, a rough, temporary resting place with two slapdash shelters fashioned of pine and balsam boughs leaning against stakes sticking up out of the ground. One Apache warrior was carrying wood past the ponies to a newly built cook fire. Clayburn counted the other men. There were no women. He counted eleven warriors in all.

From the absence of women, and the young, fit look of

each warrior, and the transient nature of their camp, they were a raiding party, out for blood and loot. But Clayburn doubted that they'd try any full attack on Cora's wagons, even if they chanced to find them. They might try sniping, though they would have nothing to gain by it but enjoyment. But as long as no wagon fell behind, and no man strayed away as Roud had done, they were likely to leave the wagon train alone. It had too many men, and with every teamster armed the numerical odds were too even. Judging from the size of the two shelters, even if all the raiding party weren't in the camp at the moment, there couldn't be more than a couple others—not including the one he'd killed.

Apache warriors gambled with their lives. But like all sensible gamblers they preferred the odds to be at least slightly in their favor before staking everything. Still—they *could* make trouble if they happened to discover the wagon train.

Clayburn was about to turn away when another Apache climbed into view over the crest of a ridge off to the right. At the same moment the newcomer looked over and spotted Clayburn.

The Apache yelled his warning to the camp below as Clayburn whirled his sorrel around, tugging Roud's horse after him. Cora's wagon train was off to the west. Clayburn raced to the east, toward the other pass.

He hadn't gotten far before he heard Apache ponies coming after him.

FOURTEEN

Ranse Blue picked the campsite for Cora's wagon train as dusk closed in. They were in a wide, level stretch of the pass now. Blue chose a place against a high, perpendicular cliff, with no timber or sizable rocks close enough to be used by night attackers. Kosta quickly saw to getting the evening meal ready, so that he'd be done with the cooking before full dark. There'd be no fire to reveal their position that night, or in the nights that would follow.

As the mules and horses were corralled within the square of wagons Cora stood by the cook fire, gazing anxiously to the east. "Why isn't Clay back yet?" The question was more of an expression of her fears than a query directed at Blue. "He should have come back by now. . . ."

"Most likely he found that Apache," Blue said, with more gentleness than he ever used with any of the men, "and decided to trail him."

"But we need him here."

"We need to know where the rest of them Apaches are, and how many, too."

"Then what about Jim Roud? . . . He hasn't come back either."

"Could be he went along with Clayburn," Blue lied, "to help in case he ran into trouble."

Kosta glanced up at Blue, saying nothing but knowing as well as Blue that it wasn't so.

Cora knew it, too. When she settled down in her bedroll that night after the meal she was thinking of Roud's cheerfully ugly face. And she found herself thinking of him already as someone in the past, not as someone who still lived.

Weariness made her fall asleep in spite of her thoughts. But it was a restless, troubled sleep.

Blue assigned the three-man guard duties for the night, and picked with forethought the position from which each guard would stand his watch. There was one natural advantage to the situation of that night's camp. No one could get at them directly from either steep-walled side of the pass. Any night attack would have to come through the pass behind them, or ahead of them. . . .

When Haycox was wakened for his turn at guard duty shortly before midnight, he saw that it was still snowing. He picked up his rifle and moved through the darkness to take up his position, the last vestige of sleepiness quickly left behind, his mind sharply alert as he reviewed his plans.

He'd thought them out nights ago, after Cora had made it obvious that she found him repulsive, that she'd played him for a sucker back there in Parrish. He'd decided that night that he would switch sides and go over to Adler. But that was not all he had decided to do. And he'd waited patiently for the right situation.

Now he had it. There were only two other guards beside himself tonight. And the falling snow would wipe out his tracks before anyone could start trailing him at dawn.

Adler would pay him triple money for changing sides. But Haycox wanted more than that. And he was quite sure Adler would pay him more—much more—for having Cora delivered to him as a hostage.

Haycox waited, watching the dark shapeless forms of the men sleeping on the ground by the wagons, giving the three men who'd just been relieved from guard duty time to get deep into their sleep. He knew the positions of the other two guards. He was fairly sure he could accomplish what he had to before either of them noticed. They weren't likely to be looking his way.

Haycox allowed a half hour to go by. Then he left his guard position and slipped away in a low crouch toward the spot where he'd watched Cora bed down. He moved slowly and quietly, making no sound as he approached her. Coming to a stop a few feet away, he studied the way her dark form lay in the shadows, locating the position of her head just showing out of the blanket wrapped around her. Then he drew one of his Colts and closed in, bending over her. He raised the gun a few inches, then whipped it sharply against the side of her head.

It was a controlled blow, not too hard. Just hard enough to knock her out instantly. She quivered, not coming out of sleep; then rolled on her back and lay still. Haycox had struck her with exactly the force he'd intended, neither more nor less. It wouldn't damage her much. She'd remain unconscious just long enough for him to get away with her.

Crouching over her, Haycox took a careful look around, saw no sign that what he'd done had been seen or heard. Sliding the Colt back into its holster, he stripped the blanket from her. She'd gone to sleep fully dressed, even to her boots, like the rest of them. Haycox got his arms under her thighs and back, and lifted her from the ground.

It was hard going, carrying Cora's inert weight. He was panting when he got her to one of the openings between the wagons. Putting her down on the ground by a wagon wheel, Haycox stood there for a few moments getting his breath back. Then he untied the ropes stretched between the two wagons. He slipped inside and walked his horse out, making as little noise as possible. His gear was close at hand where he'd placed it before bedding down. He saddled the horse with swift, efficient movements, slid his rifle into the scabbard.

He was about to go in to get another horse for Cora when a voice said quietly behind him, "What the hell're you up to?"

Haycox turned quickly, hand touching the gun on his right hip. It was one of the other guards, a teamster named Murchison. Haycox cursed himself for having become too preoccupied to notice his approach. But the teamster didn't act suspicious, only puzzled.

"Think I saw something move back down the pass," Haycox told him softly. "I'm going for a look."

"By yourself? You shouldn't . . ." The words trailed off as Murchison, glancing downward, saw Cora for the first time. "What the . . ."

Haycox already had his gun in hand and was slashing it across the other man's temple. But Murchison's cry of surprise was out, too loud, before the gun barrel struck. Even as he fell dark figures were coming up off the ground by the wagons as men were jerked out of sleep by the sound, rising to their knees and feet.

With the camp exploding awake around him, there was no longer time to get the other horse. Haycox bent quickly and grabbed up Cora's sprawled figure, slung her across his horse in front of the saddle. The next second he'd vaulted onto the horse and was racing away down the pass.

He was out of sight before anyone in the camp could begin to find out what was going on.

Clayburn rode into the other pass with the Apaches racing after him. He went across it pushing the sorrel hard all the way. The snow was getting deeper, and a couple of times the sorrel stumbled getting through heavy drifts. Once Clayburn almost had to let go of the rope that pulled Roud's horse along behind him. But he'd had a head start on his pursuers and the ground snow was slowing them, too.

He reached the other side of the pass still beyond accurate range of the Apache rifles. Working up the timbered slope there, he sped on to the east, leading the Apaches off in the opposite direction from Cora's wagon train. He kept going due east until nightfall.

With the coming of dark, Clayburn turned north, rode into a thick stand of timber, and drew to a halt. Minutes later he heard the sounds of the Apache ponies going past his hiding place, though he couldn't see them.

He waited until the sounds faded out to the east of him. Then he climbed down from the run-out sorrel. Switching to Roud's horse and bringing the sorrel along by the lead rope, Clayburn rode out of the thick timber and struck toward the south.

With the night, the falling snow, and the heavy overcast of cloud blotting out stars and moon, there was no danger of the Apaches finding his trail. And by dawn there'd be none of his tracks left in the area to tell them he'd changed direction.

Clayburn continued south for a time. Then he turned west, crossing the other pass there and heading back toward the pass his own outfit was using. It was a long ride.

It stopped snowing an hour before he reached the wagon camp. This time it had the look of not starting again for a while. The overcast was breaking up into separate clouds; stars began to show themselves. Clayburn rode into the pass and turned north. Before long he sighted the dark mass of the bunched wagons ahead.

When he was within hailing distance of the guard positions Clayburn called out, identifying himself. As he rode into the camp he saw with surprise that the whole crew was up, gathering around him swiftly. By the time he had both feet on the ground they'd told him what had happened.

It was Murchison that told him about Cora. "She was unconscious. Haycox must've knocked her out. Soon's I saw her layin' there I started to yell. Next thing I knew I was comin' to on the ground with this headache."

"We went after him," Kosta said heavily. "But he lost us. And it was too damn dark to find his trail."

Clayburn was silent for a few moments. He seemed to be gathering himself up out of his wariness. He drew a hand across his haggard face and turned to Ranse Blue. There was a hard, flat look to his stare. When he spoke his voice was soft and steady.

"Which way'd he go?"

Blue pointed south with his thumb. "Back down the pass. But he must've cut off from it somewhere. We went after him, and goin' faster than he could've with his horse carrying double. We'd've caught him if he'd stuck to the pass."

Blue glanced up at the sky. "But it looks like Haycox made a little mistake. He figured the snow'd cover his tracks. Only now it's stopped snowin' and he'll be makin' a nice clear trail. I figured at dawn a bunch of us could circle around back there till we find his back trail, and . . ."

"How long before it stopped snowing did Haycox head out?" Clayburn cut in.

"About two hours. A little less."

Clayburn shook his head. "Take a lot of time to find where his tracks start. And we can't spare the men. We're shorthanded as it is."

He told them then about Jim Roud—and the Apaches. "We're well to the west of them, and in a couple days we'll be well north of them. But meanwhile they *could* find us and make enough trouble to hold up the wagons. Especially if too many men are off hunting Haycox. I'll go after him, alone. Till I get back you're in charge of keeping the wagons on the move."

Clayburn turned to Kosta. "Fix me something to eat. And hot coffee. A lot of it."

"You said no fires at night," Kosta reminded him.

Clayburn repeated himself, "Fix me a meal. And coffee."

Kosta started to do so without another word.

"Get me two fresh horses ready," Clayburn told Blue.

The old man looked dubious. "One man alone'll take a helluva long time to find Haycox's back trail. Besides, you ain't got a chance till it gets light."

Clayburn rubbed his hands restlessly against his thighs. "I won't be hunting for his back trail. If I'm thinking straight, he's headed for Adler's outfit. Adler'd pay a lot to get Cora Sorel in his hand. He could force her to sell her freight to him, at his price, with a legal written contract. And use her to make us hand over the wagons."

Blue nodded slowly. "Could be. . . . So you figure he'll head south down the other pass to meet up with Adler's wagon train. And all you got to do is ride the same trail, only faster."

"His horse is carrying double," Clayburn said evenly,

"and I'll have two. If I sight Adler's wagons without coming across Haycox or his tracks it'll be because I've passed him. If so, I'll turn back and keep looking. One way or the other, I'm going to get to Haycox before he gets to Adler."

"*If* he's on his way to Adler," Blue put in. "You could be wrong."

"I'd better *not* be."

When Kosta had the pan of hot beans and bacon ready, Clayburn made himself eat all of it. He had no appetite, only an irritable impatience to be on his way. But he hadn't eaten since noon, and he was going to need it. He was worn out from riding and there was more riding to do. And there'd be no sleep for him this night. He gulped down scalding hot coffee without tasting or feeling it, held out the cup for a refill and drank that down too before finishing the last of his food.

As Kosta poured him a third cup, Clayburn told him to fix him a food bag sufficient for a couple days.

"I already did," Kosta said. "Biscuits, salt beef and cooked beans. And your canteen's filled, too."

Clayburn drank the rest of the coffee and rose to his feet. Blue voiced one last objection: "I still don't like the idea of you goin' after Haycox alone. That one's a real deadly breed of snake."

"I've killed snakes before," Clayburn told him, and went to the horses.

FIFTEEN

Several hours after noon Haycox came to a place where the land heaved up in a series of snow-covered hills that separated two mountain slopes a mile apart. He was on foot, leading his tired horse and pushing Cora on ahead of him. She stumbled with every other step, apparently ready to collapse.

Haycox found that his own legs were getting heavy. But the horse needed the rest from carrying them. Haycox decided to let the animal have another fifteen minutes. Then it would have to carry them again. He didn't care if it finally died from the effort, as long as it got them to Adler.

He started up the slope of a hill, prodding Cora's back hard with his fist to make her climb. She staggered up ahead of him, each step an obvious effort. When she reached the crest of the hill she let her legs give way and sat down in the snow. Drawing up her legs, she wrapped her arms around them and put her forehead down on her knees.

Haycox halted beside her and gazed south down the pass, hoping to see Adler's wagons coming toward him. They weren't in sight yet. Fingers nervously caressing the butt of one gun, Haycox turned and looked back the way he'd come. There was no one in sight there either. But he could see only too clearly the tracks he'd left behind, sharply visible all the way back to a line of trees half a mile to the north.

He hadn't figured that it would stop snowing as soon as

it had. But he consoled himself with the thought that they wouldn't have been able to start tracking him till dawn; and even then it was bound to have taken them a couple of hours to find where his trail started. He still had plenty of time to get to Adler's outfit before anyone following his trail caught up with him. He was counting on that.

Haycox looked down at Cora coldly. "Get up and get moving."

Her head remained on her knees. She gave no sign that she heard him.

"I said get up!"

Cora raised her head, but otherwise did not move. "I can't. I have to rest."

"You'll get your rest later," Haycox told her in that peculiar, empty voice of his. "And don't make me repeat my orders. If I had the time I'd teach you how to obey. You're long overdue for a rough lesson."

She almost smiled. "But you don't have the time, do you? You're scared stiff they'll catch . . ."

He slapped her, moving too fast for her to dodge it. The sound of his palm against her cheek was sharp and loud. Cora fell over on her side and lay there looking up at him. There was no fear in her face, only hate.

"You'll either get up," he told her, "or I'll start kicking you. Hard."

She got her feet under her and stood up, swaying.

But she was not as weary as she looked. She was merely doing everything she could think of to slow their progress. She had started doing so shortly after she came to on his horse during the night. Picking a place were the snow looked deep and soft, she'd fallen off the horse. That had forced Haycox to stop, climb down and pick her up. And she'd pretended to be semiconscious, going limp to make it harder for him to get her and himself back on the horse.

She'd done it again a few minutes later. After that he'd had to give a lot of his attention to holding her from falling. The rest of the time that she rode, Cora leaned all the weight she could forward against the horse's neck to tire it faster. When she walked, she staggered.

She staggered now, as Haycox pushed her ahead of him. At the bottom of the slope she dropped to her knees, head sagging.

Haycox stopped and looked at her viciously. "I meant what I said about kicking you."

"I'm too exhausted to go much farther, no matter what you do to me. And if you kick me to death I won't be worth much to Adler."

"I won't have to kill you," Haycox told her, smiling. "You're like your mules when they get a touch of the whip. You'll be surprised how a little pain can make you keep going a lot longer than you think you can."

Cora got up very slowly. They went through a short, narrow opening between two hill slopes, came out the other side. . . .

Clayburn's voice said behind them, "Stand right there."

Cora didn't have to be told what to do. She did it instantly, dropping flat to the ground to leave Haycox a clearly exposed target. Haycox whirled around, his hands flashing to the grips of his guns. He stopped himself with the guns halfway out of their holsters.

Clayburn leaned against the side of a notch in the hillslope, holding his carbine trained on Haycox's middle. Behind him, deeper inside the notch, were his two horses.

Haycox forced his fingers to spread open, letting the two Colts slide back into place in their holsters.

Clayburn straightened a bit. His eyes had a dull shine to them in a face that appeared sleepy. "Now unbuckle your guns."

Haycox remained frozen in position, hands still poised over the grips of his guns. "You're wearing a gun on your hip," he whispered tightly. "Put the rifle down and we'll both have an even chance."

"Not so even," Clayburn said without heat. "You made the mistake of showing me how fast you are."

"You're saying you're afraid of me?"

"Uh-huh. I'm afraid. Now either go for your guns or drop them. You've got two seconds to decide."

Haycox stared at the round dark eye of the carbine aimed

at his stomach. His hands went to the buckles of his gunbelts, unfastened them and let them fall to the snow.

"Now kick them away from you," Clayburn told him in the same monotonous tone.

Haycox hesitated, then hooked a toe under each gunbelt and kicked them away. "If you're going to shoot me down . . ."

"If I was going to shoot you down without a chance, I'd have done it by now. You wanted a fair duel. You'll have one."

Haycox frowned slightly. "I don't understand."

"You will."

Cora was rising to her feet. Clayburn glanced at her, seeing the imprint of Haycox's hand on her face. "Did he hurt you much?"

She touched her cheek. "I didn't enjoy it. You were near enough to hear. Why didn't you stop him?"

"He might have spotted me before I could get behind him," Clayburn explained unemotionally. "Your friend is too good with those guns. I figured you could take a slap better than I can take a bullet."

"You *are* yellow," Haycox sneered, still clinging to a faint hope of goading the other man into a fast-draw contest.

Clayburn told Cora in a lazy voice, "Move farther away from him."

Cora obeyed immediately, watching them.

Clayburn motioned at Haycox by raising the carbine an inch. "Back up three steps."

Haycox backed away slowly, like a man in a trance, not knowing what came next. Clayburn moved to Haycox's horse, drew the rifle from its saddle scabbard and checked it. He levered a cartridge into the fire chamber, thrust the rifle back into the scabbard. Then he backed off into the notch in the hillside and brought out one of his horses.

"Come back beside your horse," he told Haycox.

The puzzled look was gone from the killer's face. He moved up beside his saddle with all of his usual smooth-flowing grace. Clayburn unbuckled his own gunbelt and let it fall. Then he slid his carbine into the saddle boot of the horse beside him, and faced Haycox with his hands empty. He still looked sleepy, but something savage glowed in the depths of his green eyes.

"Understand now?"

"No." But Haycox did understand.

"You wanted to try your speed against mine," Clayburn said softly. "Let's try it with something neither of us've spent all that time practicing."

Haycox said nothing. But he took on a coiled-spring look, spreading his feet a little, his narrow shoulders hunching forward.

"All right," Clayburn whispered—and reached for his carbine.

Haycox twisted toward his horse and whipped the rifle from its scabbard. All of his fantastic ingrained speed was there. But the combination of movement and weapon was not the one he'd devoted most of the years of his life to making part of him. It took him a split second to bring the rifle to bear on Clayburn.

Clayburn shot him in that split second.

The bullet struck Haycox in the right side of his chest. It spun him completely around. His finger was on the trigger of his rifle but he suddenly could not find the power to pull it.

Clayburn, holding the carbine hip-high, fired again. The weapon jerked in his hands. Haycox was flung away. He fell on his back, arms and legs sprawling out from his body and then freezing that way. His mouth was open and so were his eyes, staring at a sky they couldn't see.

Clayburn turned his head slowly, first one way, then the other, as though easing a knot in the back of his neck.

He unfastened one hand from the carbine and lowered it.

He said in an ordinary voice, "His horse looks wore out."

"It is," Cora said shakily.

"Then we'll leave it here, with him . . . for Adler's

outfit to ponder on when they get here. Which'll be in about three hours."

He hefted the carbine in his hand, looked at it, then slid it back into his saddle scabbard.

"But take his rifle," he said, in the same even voice. "It may come in handy."

They made cold camp deep in the mountains shortly after nightfall, sharing the beans, hard biscuits and salt beef from Clayburn's food bag and washing it down with water. Clayburn ate slowly, finding it tiring to chew. Finally he gave up.

"I've had it," he announced, as much to himself as to Cora, listening to the dull sound of his own voice. "We'll have to sleep here and push on at dawn. I've been two days and a night riding without sleep."

"If it helps any," she said dryly, "I appreciate it."

Clayburn nodded aimlessly. "It's nice to know." He shoved to his feet and went slowly to get the blanket roll from one of the horses.

Later, when Cora was bedded down in the blankets, she looked up at his shadowy figure in the faint starlight filtering through the pine boughs. "How about you?" she asked him.

"I've slept cold before," he told her drowsily. But he continued to stand there, looking down at her.

Cora's lips quirked. She raised one side of the top blanket a bit. "There's room enough. And we'll both be warmer."

Clayburn sighed. "I was hoping you'd offer." He lowered himself and slid between the blankets with her, their bodies just touching.

Cora turned her head and studied his face inches from hers. "You still look all tensed."

He smiled at her. "Sometimes it takes a while to let go."

She was silent after that, looking at him meditatively. Finally she said very quietly, "I suppose I could help." She turned on her side, bringing all her soft warmth against him. "After all, you did earn this much. . . ." There was just a trace of amusement in her voice, and something else. Her hand slid behind his neck, fingers feeling their way through his hair.

Clayburn made a soft, chuckling sound in his throat, a sound of deep-down animal pleasure. His hands found her. "Sure you know me well enough now?"

"Well enough . . ." she whispered with her lips moving on his, "to want to know more. . . ."

By the time they broke camp next morning and started north again, Cora's wagon train was being destroyed.

SIXTEEN

It was late afternoon when Clayburn and Cora, riding north up the pass on the trail of her wagons, sighted the buzzards wheeling lazily around an area up ahead. Clayburn eyed the carrion birds narrowly. Without saying anything, he moved his horse along faster. Cora kept pace with him, watching the buzzards and wondering what they meant.

They found out when they reached the place over which the buzzards hovered. The pass there had high, steep walls, supporting only an occasional dwarf pine or oak. Down in the pass between these high walls was what was left of the wagon train.

One wagon lay over on its side in the middle of the pass, a back wheel broken on a sharp hump of ground stone. There were dead mules all around it. To one side the rest of the wagons had been formed into a rough fort, with the surviving mules. Nearby, a group of men were engaged in digging two graves. They straightened and stood where they were, bleakly watching Clayburn and Cora approach.

As he rode up, Clayburn looked at the two dead teamsters stretched on the ground between the grave holes. One was a long, lanky man named Kirby. The other was O'Hara, one of the new men he'd hired in Parrish.

Kosta was limping badly, one trouser bullet-ripped and blood-stained. One surviving teamster had a broken arm. Another had a bullet-gashed cheek and a torn ear.

Ranse Blue looked miserably at Cora as they dismounted. "Afraid I let you down, Miss Sorel," he said. He seemed to have aged since Clayburn had last seen him.

Cora looked dazed and sick. "How could it happen?" she demanded. Her voice trembled uncontrollably.

Clayburn answered for Blue. "Easy enough," he said harshly. "With Roud, Haycox and me gone, that left just Blue to ride guard."

Blue nodded and drew a bony hand across his mouth as if wiping away a taste he didn't like. "They were up on that ridge there," he told them, pointing. "Six of 'em, from their fire. Must've got in position there in the night. We rode right into it just after breakin' camp this morning. They concentrated on the mules."

"So I see," Clayburn said bitterly. He had counted twenty-one dead mules. He went on thoughtfully, "I had a look at Adler's wagon train yesterday. From a long way off, but I'm damn sure there weren't six men missing from his crew. Anyway, they couldn't spare that many and still handle all their wagons. Which means Adler went and got himself some more men."

Cora turned her dazed eyes to him. "Where? Where could he get more around here?"

"From Bannock. Mules pulling heavy wagons move a lot slower than men riding horses. Adler could easily get to Bannock, hire five new men, and get back down here with them in time."

"He sure picked 'em," Blue rasped. "All good rifle shots. I got Kosta and a couple of others and went up there after 'em. We got one. Found his body. The rest cut and rode off. Guess they figured they'd done what they'd come for. As much as they could do without getting caught up there."

Kosta spoke up heavily, "They most likely figured they better get to Adler's wagons, to be ready in case we decided to pull the same thing on them. . . . Which ain't a bad idea."

"Killing some of Adler's mules," Clayburn pointed out, "won't get our wagons to Bannock."

Blue shook his head ruefully. "We'll have a helluva

time tryin' to get all this freight through now. We only got enough mules left to pull five of the wagons. We got a spare wheel for that one over there. But if we spread the mules thin to pull all eight wagons, it'll be too slow going. And even if we could pile all the freight on just five wagons, it'd be the same thing. Those five'd be just too heavy for the mules to pull 'em faster'n a crawl."

Blue looked up at a sky that had become once more completely overcast. "From the looks of that, the heavy snows're gettin' ready to fall. Pretty soon every pass'll be blocked too deep to get through. We won't make it, goin' that slow."

"Then we'll have to leave three of the loaded wagons behind," Cora said stubbornly. "Come back for them after we get the other five to Bannock."

"Same trouble," Clayburn told her. "The pass'll be blocked before we could get back. The three wagons would be stuck out here all winter. By spring, Indians would have everything on them."

Cora shrugged wearily. "Then I'll have to take the loss. There's nothing else we can do."

"There's one thing. . . ." Clayburn said slowly. His right hand idly smoothed itself against the leather of his holster as he gazed south. "We can get ourselves some more mules."

Cora frowned at him. "Where?"

"From Adler."

Blue gave him a dubious scowl. "How? We ain't got enough crew left to tackle Adler's outfit. With those new men he hired he's just got too many guns for us. And this time he'd be expecting us—and ready."

"Uh-huh . . ." Clayburn had a brooding, preoccupied look. "So we'll have to divide and conquer."

Blue's face showed only puzzlement.

"Something I learned when I was scouting for the cavalry," Clayburn said absently. "Of course, we'll need help to do it."

He turned his head and looked east. "In about another day, Adler'll be almost as far north as we are, in that other pass over there. And he'll be a lot nearer to where those Apaches are camped than we are."

Blue began to get it. His grin was very nasty. "That's not such a bad idea."

"Not bad at all," Clayburn agreed, and started toward the graves. "Let's get the burying done."

When the two teamsters were under their mounds of earth and piled stone, the overturned wagon had its broken wheel replaced and was heaved upright. They used the mules that were left to pull five wagons a mile farther up the pass, away from the dead mules. Then the other three freight wagons and the chuck wagon were brought up.

When they'd finished setting up camp there, Cora turned to Clayburn. "Now what?"

"Now," Clayburn said, "we wait." He drew from a pocket a deck of playing cards and began to shuffle them with a careless, fluid ease between his strong-fingered hands. "Anybody care for some poker?"

Twenty-four hours later, Clayburn stood by his sorrel high on a timbered slope, watching Adler's wagon train come up the pass below him.

He was alone. Blue and four rifle-armed teamsters were several miles farther north, waiting; they knew what to do if he didn't get back to them in time. Cora, Kosta and the other two teamsters were back in the other pass guarding the wagons.

The slope on which Clayburn stood was very high, but not steep. Far below, the bottom of this pass was an impassable jumble of rocks and boulders. But a wide ledge near the foot of the slope formed a route for the wagons. The ledge rose higher after it passed Clayburn's position. Any beyond that, out of sight where the slope grew steep, the ledge narrowed till it was only just wide enough for a wagon. Still farther north the ledge went over a ridge and there was a wide route down to an unblocked continuation of the pass.

From Clayburn's place of concealment just under the top of the slope, the wagons and mules approaching below looked toy-sized. To have gone down any closer wouldn't have given him enough escape room. Clayburn counted the men riding guard. Two came on ahead of the first wagon. There were two on each side of the wagons, riding flank. Two more rode a hundred yards behind the last wagon.

Eight in all. At that distance they were too small to be identifiable.

Clayburn got his field glasses and focused them till the two guards riding point became clear in the lenses. One of them was Wilks. The other was Dillon.

Clayburn moved the glasses slowly along the wagons until he found Adler, riding flank on the other side. He put away the glasses and drew his carbine from its scabbard. Then he waited, watching the wagon train come closer up the wide ledge below.

When the lead wagons were almost directly under him, Clayburn braced himself against a tree trunk and brought the carbine to his shoulder. He took aim at the tiny figure of Wilks.

The distance was against him. His first shot kicked up snow between Wilks and Dillon. Both instantly wheeled their horses toward the slope. Clayburn quickly levered another cartridge into firing position, following Wilks with his sights and then leading him a fraction. He fired, levered and fired again, the two shots ringing out one on the other.

Wilks spun out of his saddle. He hit the snow and rolled, scrambling to his feet. Clutching his shoulder, left arm dangling, Wilks threw himself behind a mound by the time Clayburn levered for another shot.

Clayburn swung the carbine to fire at Dillon, who vanished into the timber below before the sights were lined up on him. Cursing, Clayburn looked for the other guards. They were all gone from the ledge on which the wagons had pulled up. Which meant they were all in the timber now, working their way up the slope toward him. It was time to get out.

Sliding the carbine back into its scabbard, Clayburn grabbed the reins and tugged the sorrel after him up the slope. The timber came to an abrupt end. Clayburn went up into the saddle and kicked the sorrel. As he went over the bare crest, guns crashed out at him from the timber below. Clayburn made it down the other side, out of sight, and raced west. The sorrel left a nice clear trail behind it in the snow.

A mile farther on Clayburn looked back over his shoulder without slowing. There were five of them racing after him. Which meant that only two of them had stayed behind to guard the wagons. So far, so good. Clayburn turned his head and concentrated on getting where he was going ahead of his pursuers.

One worry was that the five wagon guards might quit and turn back. To encourage them not to, Clayburn twice slowed his horse. Each time they got closer. It was dangerous, cutting his safety margin that thin. But it was necessary to make them believe their horses were faster than his, and would soon run him to ground. If they didn't keep after him all the way the rest of it wouldn't work.

They were still with him, gradually creeping closer, slowly narrowing the gap, when he rode through a notch and sighted the stream dead ahead of him, the stand of pine on his right. He cut toward the timber and into it. His pursuers made a great deal of noise coming into the dense woods behind him.

By then Clayburn was on the other side of it, where the timber thinned out abruptly on the rising incline. There was a tall Apache warrior between the upthrustings of rock at the top of the incline—looking directly at him.

Without slowing, Clayburn whipped out his Colt and fired. The distance was far too great for accuracy with a hand gun. The shot didn't hit its target and wasn't meant to. The Apache vanished below the other side of the incline, down toward his camp by the stream.

Instantly Clayburn wheeled to the right toward a grouping of boulders leading to a low ridge. He was in among the boulders and sliding from his horse before the five gunmen came in sight behind him. Pulling off his hat, he raised his head just enough to see the incline.

Adler's gunmen rode out of the thick timber following his trail. An instant later twelve mounted, rifle-carrying Apaches boiled up over the other side of the incline's crest.

There was a moment in which both groups reined to a sudden halt as they saw each other. Before the moment ended rifles were crashing out. Clayburn saw two Apaches and one of Adler's gunmen fall. The next instant both groups were scattering for cover, firing as they moved.

Clayburn tugged the sorrel's reins and started working his way upward behind the boulders. Keeping out of sight necessitated a number of side detours. His progress upward was slow. When he neared the ridge he allowed himself one last peek over the boulders at what was happening below.

A second gunman lay dead, sprawled face down over a rock. The Apaches were all on foot now, and each had found some form of cover—a tree, a rock, a hump or hollow in the ground. They had Adler's three remaining gunmen pinned down behind some fallen timber.

There were nine Apaches left in the fight. And Apache warriors were masters at this kind of fighting. It was not likely that any of the three gunmen would get out alive. Clayburn's sympathy for them extended only so far as hoping that all three died fighting before the Apaches got hold of them.

When he had the ridge between him and the sound of the battle, Clayburn swung up into the saddle. He rode east.

SEVENTEEN

Clayburn found Blue's horse and the horses of the four teamsters tethered in the heavy timber near a narrow trail leading to the pass. He left his own horse with them. Drawing his carbine, he headed south on foot through the dense pine woods.

A mile south he came upon Blue and the teamsters crouching behind a ridge overlooking the pass. Blue heard him first. He turned, saw Clayburn, and almost smiled.

"You're in time for the fun. Adler's wagons ain't in sight yet."

Clayburn frowned. "I hope he hasn't decided to hold still till he gets all his guards back."

"Nope. I went back down and had a look. They're comin' all right. Guess Adler figured it wasn't safe to hang around the place where you sniped at 'em. Especially while his wagon train's short on guards." Blue looked at Clayburn quizzically. "Any of those others likely to get back?"

"No."

Blue looked pleased. "That's real nice."

"We got everything ready," one of the teamsters said. He was fingering his rifle, eager to use it. "Have a look."

Clayburn climbed over the ridge with the teamsters. Blue stayed on top of it, gazing south. Below the ridge was the west side of the pass, dropping too steeply to be climbed by horses or mules. Halfway down this high west slope was the ledge along which Adler's wagons would be coming from the south. The ledge was just wide enough to take a freight wagon.

Twenty yards south of where Clayburn stood the steep slope, and the ledge, curved sharply around a bend and out of sight.

Just below Clayburn two big pine trees grew from the slope. At least it would look from below as if they still did. Actually the trunk of each had been chopped through close to the base. They still stood there, leaning out slightly over the pass, only because they were secured in position by ropes that could not be seen from the ledge.

On either side of these trees, also secured by ropes, were two log platforms. Each supported a mass of huge rocks. They were hidden from below by a judicious placement of some of the spreading juniper bushes that covered much of the slope.

Clayburn looked at his teamsters. "You've been working."

"Yeah," said one of them. "But it's gonna be worth it."

He said so with deep satisfaction. . . .

When Adler's wagon train started around the bend in the ledge, Clayburn and the others were waiting above them, concealed behind the chopped-through pines and the rock platforms.

A single point rider came around the bend into sight below first. Clayburn saw with some disappointment that he was neither Wilks nor Adler. Which meant that Wilks was probably nursing his bullet-broken arm in one of the wagons, and Adler was riding drag behind the last of his twelve freight wagons.

The point-riding guard was directly below when the horse-drawn chuck wagon came around the bend. It was followed by the first of the freight wagons, then the second. Clayburn waited tensely until the third freight wagon had gone past below him and the fourth one was nearing. Then he raised his carbine and took aim at the point rider as Blue did the same. They fired at the same time. The shots hammered the guard from his saddle and flung him over the lip of the ledge toward the pass bottom far below.

At the signal, the teamsters cut all the securing ropes. The two big trees and the released rocks went thundering down the steep slope, sending up a huge cloud of snow and dust in their wake. They crashed down on the ledge between the rear of the third freight wagon and the lead mules of the fourth one. Some of the big rocks bounced off the ledge and kept on going down toward the bottom of the pass. But enough settled on the ledge itself, together with both trees, to block it completely. The fourth freight wagon was stopped dead, and it was the only one in view behind the barrier. The rest were out of sight, back around the bend.

The driver of the chuck wagon and the men handling the four freight wagons that were in sight began pulling out of their shocked surprise. They snatched up rifles, began firing up the slope.

But Clayburn, Blue, and the four teamsters with them were also firing. And they had no surprise to pull out of before taking aim. They worked their way down toward the ledge, shooting as they went.

The chuck-wagon driver was shot out of his seat before he could do more than start to lift his rifle. One of Adler's freighters was killed in midair as he leaped toward the ground. Another was smashed off the ledge as he scrambled for cover.

The man who'd been driving the fourth freight wagon sprinted south and vanished around the bend. The only Adler man still alive on the north side of the ledge barrier dropped his rifle and Colt, stepping out from behind his wagon with his hands held high. The first of Clayburn's teamsters to reach the man knocked him cold with his rifle stock.

The teamsters were climbing up onto the wagons when Clayburn and Blue reached the ledge. Clayburn found that from there he could not see the mules and wagon on the other side of the barricade. The lead teamster got the chuck wagon moving north. The point-rider's horse had long since disappeared up the ledge at a gallop.

As the first freight wagon started up, Clayburn and Blue climbed up onto the back of the third one, watching the huge barricade of rocks and trees behind it. The second freight wagon followed the first.

Rifle barrels appeared over the top of the ledge block—then some heads started to inch up on the other side. Blue and Clayburn fired simultaneously. The heads ducked back out of sight. The third freight wagon got rolling.

The wagons picked up speed as they moved north on the ledge. In a few minutes they turned another bend. The great barrier they'd sent crashing down on the ledge could no longer be seen behind them.

A mile farther, the slope above them became much less steep. Halting, they worked swiftly at detaching the mule teams from the wagons, leaving the mules in their traces. The same was done with the chuck wagon and its horse teams. Then, one by one, they rolled each of the wagons over the ledge, sending it crashing down into the rocks below.

When the last one had gone over, Clayburn looked down at the broken wagon and scattered freight. His brief smile was a bleak one. He turned to help the others in getting the horse and mule teams up the slope.

Beyond the crest they entered a narrow trail through dense timber. A little farther on they came to where they'd left their saddle horses. The teamsters mounted theirs and continued west, pulling the teams of mules and horses after them by lead ropes, heading for the pass where Cora's wagons waited. Blue and Clayburn stayed behind, concealed on either side of the narrow trail. Ready to cut down anyone who came riding after them.

Clayburn didn't think anyone would. Adler's outfit had only a couple of horses left with which to go anywhere. Adler wasn't going to find two men willing to commit suicide by trying to catch a larger number of armed men or hit at Cora's wagon train itself.

Clayburn was fairly sure that Adler would now have to concentrate on a number of problems that had been suddenly dumped on him. It was going to take time just to remove that ledge barrier so they could continue north. Clayburn was hoping that Adler would try piling as much of his dumped freight as could be salvaged on his remaining wagons. Getting that freight up from the bottom of the pass would delay Adler still further. And the extra weight would slow his mules considerably.

What with one thing and another, Adler wasn't likely to be troubling them again between here and Bannock.

Cora's wagon train was three days from Bannock when it ran into a blizzard that lasted almost the entire day.

If it had happened while they were farther back in the mountains, still climbing through some of the difficult stretches, it would have stopped the wagons. And they would have stayed stopped for the whole winter.

But by the time the blizzard hit, the rest of the pass between them and Bannock was level, over fairly even ground. The next day they were able to get moving again, and keep moving. The deep snow cost them another day, but they managed to get through.

When they reached Bannock it didn't appear to have been worth the trouble. Just dirty tents and ramshackle log huts clustered in a notch in the mountains—with a sprinkling of more of the same on the slopes. As they entered the wide track of churned up mud and snow that served as Bannock's main street, they saw there were only two wooden structures of any size in the whole place. The first they passed was a saloon. The second they came to was a general store.

By the time they pulled to a halt in front of the general store they knew that, despite appearances, Bannock was bursting with wealth. Ragged, filthy miners crowded around the wagons. They yelled for clothes, flour, sugar, tools . . .

And they offered gold for what they demanded.

They would have stormed the wagons but for the teamsters quickly taking up positions with their rifles to stop the rush. Clayburn, directing them, found that Blue was gone.

The old man had been with them, riding drag, when they'd come into Bannock. Now he was nowhere in sight. Clayburn glanced back the way they'd come—to the big saloon at the other end of the mining camp.

The man who came out of the general store to meet Cora was as eager as the miners. He quickly assured her she'd do better to sell in bulk to him than piecemeal to the miners; warned her that her freight wouldn't be safe till it was in his store where it could be more easily guarded; and invited her to discuss the terms of the deal inside. Clayburn didn't think much of the man's chances of outdealing Cora. She was smiling at the man too innocently.

Before going into the store, she turned to Clayburn. "Mind finding out if whoever owns that big saloon back there is interested in buying some decent liquor? Tell him I've got a whole wagon full."

"How much'll you want for it?"

"Tell him I'll discuss terms with him myself, when he gets here."

Clayburn smiled admiringly at her. "You mean you *still* don't trust me?"

Her dark eyes were warm as they met his. "You *know* I do," she told him softly. "Just not where money's concerned."

With that she went into the general store. Clayburn shook his head, still smiling. Then he told his men to shoot anybody who tried to get closer to the wagons, and strode off to the saloon on the other side of Bannock.

As he'd expected, Ranse Blue was at the bar, drowning what was probably not his first whiskey. The old buffalo hunter saw him come in and immediately got a defensive look. Clayburn went past the bar without speaking to him. He found the owner of the saloon and told him about

Cora's wagon-load of liquor. The man went out as fast as he could without running.

Clayburn turned to the bar, looking at Blue.

Blue glared at him. "I said I didn't drink on the trail. And I didn't. But we're not on the trail any more, are we?"

The corners of Clayburn's mouth turned up slightly. "Do you hear me complaining?" As he turned away he added, "I may be back in a little while. I could use a good drinking session myself." He went out of the saloon.

Adler stood there outside, facing him, less than twenty feet away.

Clayburn stopped, looking at the way Adler held his right hand, close by the gun holstered on his hip. "So you got here," he said evenly.

Adler nodded slowly. "Yes, I got here." His voice was quiet, rigidly controlled. "But my wagons didn't."

"Too bad. That's why we didn't use the pass you took. I figured some of those ledge trails'd become impassable if a real blizzard hit."

"You know what it does to me?" Adler went on, his voice beginning to be edged with his held-down fury. "It means I lose every cent I put into those wagons. They'll be stuck out there all winter. Indians'll pick them clean. You did that to me, by holding me up just long enough to get my wagons stuck in that snow. You've ruined me."

"You ruined yourself," Clayburn told him coldly. "If you hadn't wasted everybody's time riding back and forth, trying to stop us, we'd *both* have got all our wagons here three-four days ago. Before the blizzard."

Adler wasn't listening. He said in the same tightly controlled, fury-driven voice, "I'm going to kill you. You know that."

Clayburn didn't believe it. Didn't believe Adler was the man to face him evenly, no matter how crazy with anger he was.

There was the blank wall of the saloon on Clayburn's right. He turned his head swiftly and looked to his left.

Wilks was there, standing in an opening between two brown-colored tents. His left arm was in a sling. There was a Colt in his right hand, pointing. . . .

Clayburn twisted to face Wilks, swerving to one side as he brought his own gun up from its holster. He'd never drawn faster. He fired at Wilks as the gun cleared leather. Wilks' shot roared a hair's-breadth later.

A small black hole appeared in the middle of Wilks' forehead, the force of the bullet knocking his hat off. Clayburn felt an enormous blow against the right side of his chest that nailed him against the saloon wall. His right arm went entirely numb. His gun hand sank as he saw Wilks topple forward.

Sagging against the wall, desperately fighting the agony in his chest and the darkness squeezing his brain, Clayburn tried to bring himself around for a shot at Adler. He saw Adler's revolver coming up out of its holster, found his own gun had become too heavy to lift with his right hand. He fumbled for it with his left hand, couldn't seem to find it. Through blurred eyes he watched Adler leveling the revolver at him.

Ranse Blue fired his rifle from the saloon doorway. The bullet smacked into Adler just below the breast bone and drove him backward. The revolver spilled from his hand. He got a look of mild surprise on his face. Then death took over the expression of his features.

Through a mist Clayburn watched him fall. Then his own legs gave way. He slid slowly down the wall until his knees touched the ground. He stayed that way, still holding the Colt in his right hand, squinting wearily at the dark shapes that moved toward him through the mists.

Clayburn sat propped up on his bed in a log-walled room, playing solitaire on the blanket spread over his legs and lower torso. He handled his right arm awkwardly, keeping it away from the bulge of the bandages under his shirt. His face was paler, leaner. But the dullness was gone from his eyes.

Wind-whipped snow swept past the room's single window. It had been doing so for two days straight.

Clayburn placed a jack on a queen. The door opened part way and Cora Sorel looked in. "Oh . . . You're awake."

"You know I am," he said in a bored voice. "It's past time for our poker game. You promised to keep me amused, remember?"

She closed the door and came to the bed. "I was talking over a business deal with Feeney—the man who owns the big saloon."

"You're too damn money hungry. You could soothe your soul by spending more time with a sick man."

Cora looked at him gravely. "Dr. Judd says you're getting better fast. He expects you up and around in a couple more days."

Dr. Judd was actually a dentist who added to his income with doctoring and part-time bartending. But he'd gotten the bullet out, and Clayburn was still alive.

"A lot he knows," he grumbled. "I'm still weak as a baby. What's he predict about this blizzard?"

Cora sat on his bed, smoothly gathering up the cards into a deck. "The old-timers around here say we're all going to be stuck in Bannock for at least a month. Horses won't be able to get in or out until the snow packs down hard enough to travel on. That's the reason for my business discussion with Feeney this morning."

She shuffled the cards with a flowing motion of her slender fingers. "As long as we're going to be stuck here, I thought I might as well run my profits up a little higher. I've bought the gambling concession in Feeney's saloon. And since this is a rough place for a woman to run gambling on her own, I thought you might be interested in going partners with me."

She looked at him the way she had that night when they'd camped out alone together under the pines. "We make a good team," she reminded him softly, and began dealing out two poker hands.

Clayburn noticed that she was absentmindedly dealing every other card from the bottom of the deck.

They smiled at each other.

It just might be, Clayburn agreed, an interesting way to spend a snowbound month.